FIGHT DIRTY

BLACK ROSE KISSES #1

EVA ASHWOOD

I FUCKING LOVE FIGHT NIGHTS.

The warehouse is packed as we make our way in, weaving through little knots of people all jammed in together like sardines. The tension in the air is high, and the excitement is thick enough that it feels palpable, everyone ready for another thrilling night of fights.

It's the perfect place to house a bareknuckle boxing ring. The warehouse is nondescript and out of the way enough that only the die-hard fans and participants find their way out in the middle of the night to see the matches.

Scarlett's at my side like she always is. Like she always has been. We grew up together, living in rough neighborhoods and making the best of sometimes shitty situations. Nothing in our lives has ever come easy, but we've always had each other. And we've come out of it all tougher, with a bond that's unbreakable.

When someone knocks into her as we pass, she shoves him back and then gives a look that dares him to say anything about it. Her sweet face is deceptive as hell, but whatever the guy sees in her eyes makes him hold up his hands and back off.

She shoots me a satisfied smile, and we keep moving.

"I'll find us a spot to watch from if you want to go on back," Scarlett says once we've pushed through the worst of the crowd.

She knows the routine well since she's usually with me whenever I come out on fight night. If she were anyone else, I might worry about leaving her alone with the kind of people who come to watch the brutal spectacle these events usually are, but Scarlett can more than handle herself. So I give her a grin and slip off to the back to find my dad.

Ever since my mom died when I was seven years old, it's just been me and Dad. He's all the family I really know, and every time he has a fight, I find him in the locker room beforehand to wish him luck.

He's stretching when I walk in, and I grin, waiting for him to notice me. He punches at the air a few times, warming up, then turns to smile at me, eyes crinkling at the corners.

"There she is," he says warmly. "My good luck charm."

He's called me that for as long as I can remember, asking me to pick lotto numbers for him or blow on his dice

2

before a game. Maybe it's dumb, but it gives me the same sense of pride at twenty as it did when I was a little kid.

"How're you feeling about tonight?" I ask him, perching on the bench in front of rows of identical lockers painted an ugly shade of green.

Dad shrugs a shoulder and then rolls it. "About the same as always. You never know how it's going to go until you get in the ring. Overconfidence is a killer."

"You always say that." I smirk, rolling my eyes. "And yet you always win."

He cocks an eyebrow at me. He's got the same dark hair I do, and I know I got it from him, just like my green eyes. My mom had dark blonde hair and blue eyes. "That's because I keep my head together and don't go in thinking the fight's won before it's even started."

"Just make sure you keep your head out of the way of their fists," I counter with a smirk. "Keep 'em on their toes. Heel of the hand so you break *their* bones, not yours."

Dad gives me a look that's a cross between exasperated and proud. "Who do you think you're talking to, Mercy?" He chuckles, running a hand over the light stubble on his jaw. "I'm the one who taught you all that."

"I know." I affix an innocent expression to my face. "I'm just making sure you haven't forgotten in your old age."

He snaps a towel at me, and I jump up from the bench to avoid it, laughing with him. At thirty-eight, my dad *is*

3

one of the older fighters still competing. Sometimes I worry about him a little when he goes up against one of the younger, up-and-coming guys. But he's still one of the best fighters out there, not just because of his strength and skills, but because he fights smart.

"Come here, you little brat." Dropping his towel on the bench, he catches me in a one-armed hug that I return with a smile. "Thanks for the pep talk. I'll take your advice to heart. Now get out of here before someone comes in."

I take *his* advice and slip back out the way I came, side-stepping a burly looking man as I make my way back to the main part of the warehouse and the clusters of people packed around the ring.

I have to stand on my toes to see where Scarlett is standing, firmly guarding the little pocket of space that she's picked out for us. Before I can get all the way over there, a group of three guys pushing their way through the throngs of people catch my eye.

They're the typical type I'd expect to see at something like this. Tall, well-built, oozing confidence, and sexy as fuck. All three of them look like they could be models if they wanted to, although I'm sure none of them actually do. They walk through the crowd like they own the whole damn place.

It's not until they get a little bit closer that I realize I know one of them. Rich brown eyes, dark hair, cheek-bones for days, and a jaw that looks like it was hand-

crafted to break hearts and fists. I have to stop myself from staring.

Oh, shit.

A hand wraps around my wrist, yanking me out of my momentary daze, and Scarlett tugs me over to her, reclaiming the spot she vacated before anyone else can snag it. She shoots me a curious look, obviously reading the expression on my face, then turns her head to follow my line of sight.

Her eyebrows raise when she catches a glimpse of the guys, who are farther away in the crowd now. "Oh, hey, isn't that the dude you hooked up with?"

"Yeah," I murmur, my gaze still locked on him. "Levi."

About a year ago, Levi Hendrix and I hooked up once. It was hot and intense in the best way; his hands all over me, pinning me down to the wall, the bed, the floor. Even thinking about it now has me flushing with heat, and I rip my focus away from him and his friends, not wanting to catch their eyes.

Levi is a member of the Black Roses gang, and I can only assume his two buddies are as well. I knew it was probably stupid to hook up with him, but when I met him at a house party last year, he caught my eye immediately. We eye-fucked and flirted for about half an hour before we ended up in a bedroom upstairs, tearing at each other's clothes. We stayed in that room until dawn, and it was hands down one of the best nights of my life.

5

"God, they're hot as hell," Scarlett says, still eyeing them up as they move a bit further away. "The things I'd do to go a few rounds with them in the ring, if you know what I mean." She grins at me, elbowing me in the side.

"Yeah, I think everyone in a four foot radius knows what you mean, Scar; you're practically drooling all over yourself. Stop staring."

I have to reach up and physically turn her head around to face the ring to get her to stop looking in the direction the three of them walked in.

"You can't blame a girl for having eyes," she shoots back, still grinning. Luckily the lights lower, indicating that the fight is about to start, so I don't have to answer her.

My focus is immediately on the ring. Whenever my dad fights, I can't look at anything else. I watch his movements, the way he carries himself and flows from punches to blocks to ducks, almost like I'm right there in the ring with him.

The announcer riles the crowd up, whipping them into a frenzy. He calls out Dad's name—Oscar DeLeon—drawing out each syllable. My dad walks out, looking calm and collected as always, and I grin. When I was younger, I used to wave, even though he couldn't really see me in the crowd. It's enough that he knows I'm here rooting for him though.

His opponent comes out from the other side, a big dude with tattoos and wild eyes, and I size him up. If I'm

being honest, he looks a bit like the Hulk. Thickly muscled and kind of stocky, even with the three or four inches he has on Dad. Pound for pound, he looks like he could take Dad, but weight and size aren't everything.

Still, when the fight starts, it starts with a bang. The guy is aggressive right out of the gate, aiming a punch that Dad barely blocks. When Dad strikes back out, going for the dude's nose, it's blocked, and he's pushed back.

The intensity is immediate and so captivating I can't look away. Usually it's pretty easy to tell who's going to have the upper hand once a couple minutes have passed, but it's not that easy here. It's close from the get-go, the two of them trading blows with savage intensity.

Whenever Dad lashes out, his opponent is right there, ready to block, and the hits each of them *do* manage to land ring out through the warehouse, the sound of fists on faces, the crunch and crack of calluses and bones.

Neither of them are fragile, but by the five minute mark, they're both banged up. Blood drips from the guy's nose—Milo Guzman, the announcer said his name was—and my dad is already sporting a bruise around his eye that's going to turn into a hell of a shiner. The crowd around us shouts and jeers, calling out encouragement to both of them, depending on who they're pulling for.

"Kick his ass!" I practically scream, joining in the chaos. I like to imagine my dad can hear me, my voice cutting through the din of a thousand other screaming fight fans, but I know that's mostly just wishful thinking.

"The bigger they are, the harder they fall!" Scarlett yells, stomping her feet, and I grin at her for a second before turning my attention right back to the ring.

Maybe it's the energy of the crowd, or maybe a few solid punches to the face have made the big guy wake up, but he starts circling Dad, eyes narrowed. He inhales with a wet sound and then spits a glob of blood and phlegm off to the side, ruining someone's night for sure.

Dad doesn't back down, cracking his knuckles and dropping into a defensive stance right when the Hulk wannabe launches at him, raining blow after blow down on him.

My chest goes tight as I watch him take those hits. Each one sends him staggering back, and I reach down to grip Scarlett's hand. It's almost like I can feel each punch landing, shock and anger jolting through me.

"Come on," I hiss through my teeth, tightening my grip on Scarlett. "Come on. Get him the fuck off you."

Dad goes down to one knee for a second, and it's like time stops. The rip-off Hulk grins, teeth bloody and red, and stalks forward confidently. He looks like he's going to go in for the KO.

But before Milo can raise his fist for the final blow, Dad surges up to his feet, getting his bearings back.

He gives back every hit he took twice over, aiming for

the most sensitive spots on the guy's body, making him double over in pain. With one last right hook, he lays the guy out at the last second.

Milo Guzman's head whips to the side, his eyes already rolling back in their sockets as his body goes down like a sack of bricks. He hits the heavy mats inside the ring with a thud, and a roar goes up from the crowd.

The announcer slips into the ring, raising my dad's hand in the air. "Winner! Oscar DeLeon!"

Finally, I feel like I can breathe again.

Dad lifts his other hand in the air as the crowd screams its approval or its disappointment, and discount Hulk just lies there in a heap.

There's definitely going to need to be some clean up when Dad finally makes it back to the locker room, but he looks proud of himself, and I can feel that same pride swelling in my own chest.

This is the man who taught me basically everything I know, and he's still got it. Not even towering muscle bags can knock him out. I cheer at the top of my lungs, clapping and hooting, stomping my feet along with the rest of the crowd.

People at these fights are always looking for a good show, but they seem particularly bloodthirsty tonight, reveling in the brutality of the fight. If they wanted bloodshed, then they got it, and when the refs come to haul Hulk dude up and out of the ring, his face looks kind of like ground beef. That seems to set the crowd off more, people screaming in joy and fury, but I'm just glad my dad won.

I glance over to the spot where I last saw Levi and his cronies, mostly to see if they look happy or disappointed with the outcome and if they're as hungry for violence as the rest of the crowd seems to be, but they're gone, other people already surging in to take their spots.

With the show over, the rest of the crowd starts to trickle out, heading out into the comparative coolness of the night air, still giving each other blow-by-blows and discussing other things they could get into with the rest of their night.

Scarlett and I follow, letting the stream of people carry us out.

A breeze ruffles my hair as we step into the cool night air. It never gets all that cold in Fairview Heights, not even during the dead of winter. We've had a mild January so far, and the crisp breeze feels good. It cools the sweat on my neck as I push my dark hair out of my face.

"You heading out?" I ask Scarlett. She's fanning herself again, but from the temperature this time and not some hot guys.

"Yeah." She shoots me a look. "You'll be good here?"

I nod. I'm always good. "Of course. I'll wait for Dad and then head out."

She hugs me like she always does, even though we see

each other or talk on the phone almost every day, and I watch her head off to where she parked.

Usually, it only takes Dad a few minutes to clean up and patch up any injuries and head out, but as the flood of people leaving the warehouse slows to a trickle, I get antsy. He took some pretty bad hits before his comeback at the end. Maybe he needs help taking care of whatever injuries he sustained. None of them looked like anything worse than he's had before, but it was hard to tell from where I was standing in the crowd.

I could hang out here and wait, or I could go in and see what's up—and I've never been the waiting around type. So I head back inside the now-empty building and make my way back to the locker room. I expect to find him with ice on his eye or something, going over the fight in his head, dissecting what he could've done differently.

When I walk into the locker room, he's there, all right.

But he's not alone.

He's in the center of a group of guys, getting the absolute shit beat out of him.

2

My heart lurches.

Without even thinking, I run into the room. I don't care about my own safety or the fact that even with my help, we'll both be outnumbered. All I know is I have to stop these fuckers from hurting my dad.

I lunge in, grabbing one of them by the shoulder and spinning him around to face me. He looks surprised, and I take advantage of that, punching him right in the nose and then aiming my knee for his crotch. He manages to deflect that last hit somehow, even still reeling from the solid hit to his face, but I don't let up.

Taking advantage of an opponent's distraction is a great way to deal with someone like this, so much taller and thicker than me. I've been fighting guys bigger than me since I was a kid, and I know how to hold my own.

He lashes out, aiming to grab at my hair, and I duck

down under his arm and elbow him hard in the gut, relishing the grunt of pain and the way he wheezes when he hunches over.

There's still too many of them though, and taking out one guy isn't enough. They're all piling in on Dad, hitting him like they want to kill him, and I can feel that fear biting at me, urging me to do *something*.

So I abandon my fight with the first guy and shove my way through the men gathered around my dad. I throw myself in front of him, putting my body between him and his attackers.

"Stop! Leave him the fuck alone!" My voice is harsh, and I shift into a stance that makes it perfectly clear I'm ready to keep fighting to protect him.

But before I can do anything else, strong hands latch onto my arms, dragging me out of the cluster and away from my dad. Someone forces my arms behind my back, and I recognize Levi and one of the guys he was with before during the fight. They're standing in front of me, and I'm guessing Levi's other friend is the one who's got ahold of me.

"What the fuck? Let me go!" I yell, kicking and thrashing, trying to get away from them and back to protecting my father. But I don't have the element of surprise anymore, and Levi's friend hauls me up and into his grip, locking his arms around me tight enough that I can't get free.

"Well, she's a fucking handful, isn't she?" the one holding me says, sounding cheerful about it for some reason.

I narrow my eyes and keep kicking, trying to aim my foot back and hit him in the balls with it to give him something to be fucking cheerful about.

"Let's just get her out of here, Rory," Levi mutters. He doesn't look at me as he helps his buddy restrain me, and together they haul me out of the building.

I half expect them to let me go outside, or to knock me out or something so they can go back to beating the fuck out of Dad, but instead they bring me to a car. It's all black with tinted windows, the kind of car people drive when they have too much money or something to hide. I think about trying to run away if they let me go, but Levi's buddy, Rory, just drags me into the back seat with him, moving me around like I don't weigh anything.

He's the most muscular of the two Levi was with, taller than both of them and towering over me, even though at five-eight, I'm not short for a woman. The hands that grip my wrists together may as well be steel cuffs for all the leverage I can get, and I'm pulled unceremoniously into my captor's lap and held there.

I throw my head back, trying to catch the bridge of his nose with the back of my skull, but he ducks his face out of the way at the last second. I manage to catch him with a hard elbow in the side, but even though he lets out a pained grunt, he doesn't loosen his grip.

"You're a feisty thing," he mutters, and with how close he is, I can feel his breath huffing warm against my ear. "You know, in another circumstance I'd find that pretty hot."

"Fuck you," I spit, letting my fury bleed into my voice. "Let me go."

"Mm, nah. I don't think I will," he teases, and I can feel my rage mounting.

Breathing hard, I finally stop struggling in his grip. My hair is sticking to my face with sweat from the exertion, and my heart races, but I'm no closer to breaking free. And even if I could, I'm in a car with these two goons, stuck in the back seat with one of them. There's nowhere to fucking go.

As soon as I have the thought, the car's engine revs and it starts moving. My heart crawls up my throat, and I strain in Rory's grasp to peer out the window at the warehouse as we pull away.

"What's going to happen?" I blurt, addressing anyone who will answer me. "What are you doing with my dad?"

There's a moment of silence, and then Levi speaks up from the driver's seat. "I wouldn't worry about that."

"What the fuck is that supposed to mean?" I snap. "He's my *father*."

Levi sighs. "He shouldn't have crossed us," he replies. "It's not going to end well for him."

I don't need him to elaborate on that. There aren't many things his words could mean other than the obvious, and I feel my stomach drop out.

Fuck. Fuck. Fucking *fuck*.

They're going to kill him. I have no idea what my dad has gotten himself involved in, but there's no way it's anything good. These are the kind of people who play for keeps, and he's managed to get on their bad side.

From the front seat comes the trilling sound of a phone ringing, and Levi takes one hand off the wheel to dig into his pocket and pull it out.

"Yeah?" he answers, and I can just barely make out the sound of a deep male voice from the other end. Levi's quiet for a second, listening, and then he nods. "Okay."

Without another word, he hangs up and turns the car in a different direction at the next exit.

I don't recognize the streets as we go down them, and we end up at a place that looks like it might have once been an old gas station or something. There are pumps outside and a little convenience store type place with boarded-up windows. There's another car parked around the back, and before I can ask what's going on, I'm being dragged out of the car like a sack of potatoes and pushed in front of Rory.

He keeps that same tight grip on me, his arms wrapped around me and his large body crowding mine, looming tall behind me. I huff, irritated. But I don't fight back. I'm not stupid. Even if I could manage to break his grip, I'm in the middle of nowhere with no ride. If I try to run, he'll probably just shoot me in the back.

Levi holds the door open, and Rory muscles me inside. The interior is dark and dusty, but obviously not abandoned the way it looks from the outside. The men usher me through the empty storefront and into a large room at the back. It probably used to be a storeroom or something, but it's pretty much empty now too, except for the people in it.

I let out a sigh of relief when I catch sight of Dad, slumped in a chair and looking worse for wear, but alive.

"Dad!"

Instinct overrides everything else, and I try to jerk free of Rory's grip to go to him, but he's as unyielding as he was in the car, holding me back.

"Mercy." Dad's voice is raspy as he looks up at me.

The little crow's feet at the edges of his eyes crinkle up as he grimaces, his lips pulling back in a pained expression. Blood trickles down one side of his face from a cut near his eye. He looks worn down and sad, but he doesn't make a move to get up.

He's not alone in this place. There are at least six other men in the room, most hanging back, watching with sharp eyes. Two men stand over Dad though, and I take a second to look them over.

They're both definitely threats. The first is younger, a few years older than me, give or take, and a good bit taller. He's closer to Rory's height than Levi, and he's one of the two who were there with Levi at the fight. He's handsome, stupidly so, with broad shoulders, a narrow waist, and the kind of facial definition I associate with male models, not gangsters.

The other man is older and a bit shorter than the first guy, but there's something similar in the way they carry themselves. The hair and eye colors are different—this guy has brown hair and blue eyes, while the younger one is dark blond with eyes that gleam a sharp, steely gray—but it wouldn't surprise me if they're related. The Black Roses have spent years building up their power and control in Fairview Heights, so it makes sense that there's an older generation and a younger generation of gang members. Guess these things run in the family.

It's the older man who seems to be calling the shots here, his arms folded and eyes neutral as he looks down at Dad impassively.

"What the fuck was that, DeLeon? We had an agreement." He shakes his head, his eyes narrowing just slightly. "You had one job tonight. You promised us that you would throw the fight, and you managed to fuck that up. You broke your word to us, and I'm sure you know how that usually goes."

A couple of the men at the back finger their weapons

threateningly, and I can barely hear the low words from the boss man over the frantic beat of my heart in my chest.

The man smiles, and it's not a kind one. "I think I know why you did it, although that doesn't make me any more inclined to forgive you. But in light of everything, we've decided to let you live if you do something for us."

There's a beat of silence, and my gaze darts around the room, trying to get a read on what's going on here. Do something for them? What do they want him to do?

Dad stares up at the man for a long moment, and even though I can usually read my father like a book, I can't guess what he's thinking right now. I don't understand any of this, but I can practically taste the danger in the air.

It's a miracle the Black Roses haven't killed him yet, but this could still easily turn on a dime. He could die. *I* could die.

As if my thoughts somehow draw his attention, my dad's gaze shifts to me. The muscles in his cheeks ripple as he clenches his jaw, his lips pressing together. Then he sighs and turns back to the boss man, nodding his head. "Fine. Tell me what you want."

"I will," the man says. "And once you do what we ask, *if* you do what we ask, we'll consider your debt cleared. But we're keeping your daughter—Mercy, is it?—until you manage to fulfill your promise."

Dad's eyes go wide, fury burning in their depths. He opens his mouth, probably to argue, but the man just shakes his head and holds up a hand. For the first time since I entered the room, I see true anger on the man's face.

"Save it, DeLeon," he orders. "We know you're untrustworthy now, so we need a guarantee that you're not going to fuck things up the way you did tonight. Apparently, you need a little extra incentive not to double-cross us. So we'll make that part easy for you." His gaze flicks to me, his voice hard. "We'll keep her as collateral."

3

"No." Dad's voice is firm, his nostrils flaring. "No! She's not—"

Before he can continue, I step forward as much as I can with Rory still holding me back, my jaw set. "Yes. Okay. I'll do it. I'll go with you."

"Mercy, no!" Dad's words are more urgent now, and he looks like he might try to get up and fight, no matter how stupid and reckless that would be. "This was my mistake. I fucked up. You shouldn't have to—"

"Dad, it's okay." I cut him off again, desperate to get him to stop talking and calm down before he ends up with a bullet between his eyes. I don't *want* to go with these men, but if it keeps my dad alive and gives him a chance to get out of this mess, I'll gladly do it.

Besides, the guy said "collateral." That makes it sound

like they're planning on keeping me alive, at least. I'm no good as a bargaining chip against my dad if I'm dead.

"I'd listen to your daughter, DeLeon. She sounds a lot smarter than you. She might just save your life."

The older man smiles as he speaks, and Dad shoots me a look that just about breaks my fucking heart. Anger and regret churn in his green eyes, one of which is badly bloodshot, the skin around it swelling into a puffy mass. His head droops slightly, making me wonder again about his injuries. He had a tough fight and then got fucking jumped by almost a half-dozen guys, and I hope like hell that he's okay.

He looks tired and defeated, like he knows there's no way out of this for either of us. I want to ask him what this is all about, but I know there won't be time.

"Fine," he says again. "But let me have a minute with her. Please."

I'm expecting them all to disagree, but instead, Rory lets me go at a nod from the one in charge, and they all draw away a bit, not letting us out of their sight but giving us some semblance of privacy. That's more than I would have expected from assholes like this.

I can tell Dad's hurt from the way he limps over, and the bruises on his face are probably only the tip of the fucking iceberg. But he puts his hands on my shoulders and looks into my eyes.

"Fuck, Mercy. I'm so sorry. I never meant for you to get

dragged into this," he murmurs. "Be careful. Please. I know you're smart and quick, but—"

"It's okay. I'll be fine," I promise him, leaning in to give him a hug that hopefully doesn't hurt him too badly. "Just worry about *you*. Do whatever they want you to and get them off your back, okay?"

The Black Roses aren't known for being lenient, and second chances are almost unheard of. It's a miracle Dad got one, and there definitely won't be a third.

"I love you." His voice is strained as he hugs me tightly, and it feels so much like saying goodbye that my stomach twists.

"All right, let's go. We need to move," Levi says, coming back over and interrupting the moment. Once again, he's flanked by his two buddies, and Rory winks at me when I glare at all of them. For someone so big and covered in tattoos, he acts like a giant puppy, and it's fucking grating.

They don't grab me, at least, I guess trusting that now that Dad is cooperating, I'll have to do the same. And they're right. If I run, there's no guarantee they won't just kill him anyway, so I let them lead me back outside to the car.

I keep my head up and my back straight, not letting any of it show on my face, but I'm fucking pissed and scared.

Fairview Heights is ruled by two gangs, the Black

Roses and the Jackals, and they both have reputations for being brutal as hell. Probably well-earned. I know there's a pretty damn good chance my dad won't survive this, and thinking about that makes me want to punch out all three of these assholes, run back in there, and try to drag my dad to safety.

But we'd both end up getting shot if I did that. Bringing down the wrath of the rest of their gang would be a stupid idea, so I just clench my jaw and keep walking. What else can I do at this point? I agreed to go with these guys to keep my dad safe, and no matter how much I hate it —and I *really* fucking hate it—I have to go through with it.

"You know," Rory drawls as we get to the car and he opens the door for me, this time letting me slide in on my own. "She's pretty impressive. Not just anyone could dive into a fight like that and come out of it in one piece. She didn't even hesitate. Pretty fucking badass, if you ask me."

I glare at him harder, irrationally annoyed by the compliment and by the fact that he's talking about me as if I can't even hear him.

Levi snorts under his breath as he reads my expression. "Maybe you should be careful before she takes out all her badassness on you. You wanna drive, Sloan?"

The third one shrugs but goes around to the driver's side, leaving Levi to take shotgun.

Sloan is quiet for the entire drive, fingers tight on the steering wheel, looking like he's glaring out at the road and the other drivers. There's a surly air about him, like one wrong move will have him lashing out, ready to bite like a rabid dog.

Levi is more easy going, but harder to get a read on. He's still as gorgeous as he was the night we hooked up, still laid back, and other than responding to Rory or getting grunts from Sloan, he seems happy to fuck around on his phone and look out the window.

Rory, on the other hand, won't shut up.

"So," he asks, leaning into my personal space in the back seat. The gold highlights in his brown hair glint under the light of the passing streetlamps. "How'd you learn to fight like that?"

"None of your business," I snap back, folding my arms and shoving myself as far into the corner as I can to stay away from him. They're all acting so fucking casual, like they didn't just basically abduct me and threaten to kill my fucking father.

Anger burns under my skin, and I want to scream at them, but I keep it inside.

None of that seems to phase Rory a bit, and he laughs, his moss-green eyes somehow bright even in the darkness of the car. "Prefer to stay mysterious, huh? That's okay. I like a mystery, and I bet I can figure you out." He slides his gaze over my body, not even trying to hide the fact that he's checking me out.

Usually, some hot guy looking me over like he wants to

eat me alive would get my blood rushing a bit, giving me a little thrill. I've been living with my dad while I go to school, but that doesn't mean I'm some sheltered virgin or a saint.

I know I'm attractive, and I don't exactly dress like someone who doesn't want to stand out. My hair is thick and a little wavy, tumbling over my shoulders, and the rich dark chocolate color only makes my eyes stand out more, highlighting the deep shades of jade in them. I'm usually in jeans and a t-shirt for comfort, showing off part of the tattoo on my arm, and years of training and working out have added lean muscle to my soft curves.

I probably look like a bit of a mess from thrashing around and fighting, but Rory doesn't seem to have any problems with that as he eyes me up.

I look out the window and ignore him until we get to where we're going.

Somehow, I'm surprised when I recognize my neighborhood. We pull up in front of Dad's house a few minutes later, and we all get out.

I don't even bother to ask how these assholes know where I live. I also don't spare a second to worry about what the neighbors might think if any of them happen to be up and looking out their windows at this time of night to see me being escorted into my house by three men. It's none of their damn business anyway.

My burly keepers stand by the door, waiting for me to

let us all in, and then follow me to my room.

"Pack up," Sloan says shortly. "Clothes, whatever else you need. You're not coming back here until it's all said and done."

I grit my teeth, this close to telling him to go fuck himself, and then grab a ratty suitcase from the closet. It's unnerving to have the three of them standing around while I go through my dresser and pick out shirts and shorts and leggings. Rory is definitely watching when I grab a handful of underwear from one drawer, and I shove it into the bag before he can make some flirtatious comment that will make me want to punch him in the face even more.

Levi stands against the wall, not paying much attention to either the room or me, but Sloan and Rory seem perfectly happy to make themselves at home, looking around, sitting on my bed, poking at the pile of textbooks on my nightstand.

"Do you *mind?*" I ask acidly, snatching the books up and shoving them into my backpack.

"Not at all," Rory replies, grinning. Sloan just rolls his eyes, and I make myself pack faster. I don't want them here, looking at my shit, poking at the life I've built for myself in this little house with my dad. It may not be much, but it's *mine*, and I don't want their damn fingers all over it.

Leaving them alone in my room for a second, I go to the bathroom to throw some things in my smaller bag.

Shampoo, conditioner, face wash. Just the basics. Anything else, I can just buy if I need it, and I'm already more than ready to get out of here.

Or to get *them* out of here, really.

On the way out of the house and back to the car, I pause by the garage. Parked inside is the small motorcycle that I bought and fixed up a year ago. The idea of riding that to wherever we're going is way more appealing than being shoved back into the car with Rory's teasing and the silence of the other two.

"What's the hold up?" Rory asks, peering past me at the closed garage door.

"I want to ride my bike to wherever you plan to keep me," I respond, trying to sound firm about it.

"No," Sloan says immediately. "Not happening."

"What? Why not?"

"You think we're that stupid?" He narrows his eyes, leveling a flat look at me.

"What am I gonna do, run off?" I snap. "Flee across the border to Mexico? You've got my dad by the balls for whatever reason. I'm not going to abandon him."

He just shakes his head and keeps walking back to the car, and the other two follow suit, leaving me there seething.

"We'll send someone to pick it up and bring it to the house later," Levi offers, like it's some kind of olive branch.

I flip off his back and sigh, following them to the car. I

don't have any other choice, clearly.

The car ride is at least pretty short, and Rory seems to have finally exhausted himself of flirtatious jokes. Either that or he's just resting until he gets his second wind, but I'm fine with the silence either way. It's better than the teasing.

I keep my arms folded and stare out the window, but I don't recognize the neighborhood at all. The trees and houses that whip by are a good distraction from my three captors, and I focus on the scenery instead of them, still stewing in anger and worry.

This is so fucked up. The Black Rose gang shouldn't be able to control people's lives like this. They shouldn't be able to get away with basically forcing Dad to do their dirty work.

It's bullshit, and the fact that I have no choice but to go along with them if I want to keep Dad safe makes me want to hit something. Preferably one of their faces. Or all three of them. I'm not picky.

But my rage isn't productive, and it won't do anything to help Dad with the problem he has now.

Maybe there *is* something I can do to help though.

These men said they're keeping me as collateral. From the sounds of it, I'll be living with all three of them. I have no idea exactly what that will entail or how much freedom I might have in this new arrangement, but I do know one thing.

I'll be behind enemy lines.

They're all thinking of me as a captive, a pawn. But maybe, if I'm smart and play my cards right, I can be something else too.

A spy.

I don't know too much about the Black Roses, except that their business is dangerous and illegal, and most people in Fairview Heights are afraid of them. But maybe this will be a chance for me to find out more about how they operate. Maybe I can find some weakness in their organization or dig up some dirt on them that I can use as leverage.

Determination settles into my chest at the thought, slowing my pounding heart and clearing my head a little.

If no one stands up to these assholes, they'll just keep walking all over us. They'll make demands and back them up with the threat of violence, and who's going to stop them? Who's to say that even after Dad completes this job for them, they'll actually let him go?

They could keep insisting that he owes them, demanding more and more until they finally kill him anyway when he's no longer useful.

These men clearly have no honor. So the only way to ensure our protection is to learn their secrets, figure out what makes them tick.

And then I can make them pay for all of this.

I can find a way to bring the Black Roses down.

4

AFTER ANOTHER TEN minutes of driving, we pull up to a house, and it's just as annoying as everything else about these guys.

The place is gorgeous, for one thing. Big and expensive, set back from the street with a sprawling lawn that they probably have no idea how to maintain themselves. I highly doubt any of them spend their weekends out under the sun pushing a lawnmower, the way I remember my dad doing on Saturdays in the spring and summer.

They have their fancy-ass cars with the tinted windows, this fucking mansion of a house, everything they could ever want, probably, and they still throw their power around to wreck people's lives. People like my dad, who has just been trying to earn a fucking living with his fights, since that's the thing he knows best.

It makes me sick, and I glare up at the house as we get

out of the car once again. I grab my bags from the trunk, my posture and facial expression daring one of the men to try to take them from me, and for once none of them take the bait.

Levi takes charge once we're inside. "Come on," he says. "I'll show you your room."

Gritting my teeth, I follow him up the stairs without a word.

Of course the room is as nice as the rest of the house. There's a big bed in the center, the headboard placed under a window with the curtains drawn. In the daylight, it probably lets in a lot of light, filling the large space with sunshine.

I hate it anyway.

There's a dresser off to one side, a desk against the opposite wall, with a large, comfortable looking chair pulled up to it. A door next to the desk stands open, and I peek in to see an attached bathroom, complete with a tub that's clean and big enough to soak in.

"Are there cameras in here?" I ask him, dropping my bags on the floor and turning my glare on him. "So you three can get a free show to go along with me being held prisoner here? I mean, why else would you have a girl come live with the three of you, unless you're expecting something?"

He frowns and then snorts, but it's not an amused

sound. "Trust me, Mercy, none of us are that hard up for pussy. I can get laid anytime I want."

His rich brown eyes have been neutral so far, but they turn heated as he looks at me, his gaze practically burning my skin.

Immediately, I'm reminded of our hookup. I couldn't stop thinking about it for days afterward, and it's featured in an embarrassingly high number of my fantasies over the past year. I've made myself come with my own fingers more times than I can count thinking of his big hands on my waist, and the way he loomed over me and drove into me hard and fast enough to take my breath away.

My face flushes at the memory of it, and I dart my tongue out to lick my lips. And then on the heels of all that comes the realization that he's probably hooked up with countless other girls since then.

Irritation flares in me, and I can't tell if I'm irritated at him for the girls he's fucked or at myself for caring. Maybe it's a bit of both, but either way, I shove the emotion down.

I shouldn't care.

It shouldn't fucking matter who he sleeps with, and the last thing I should be doing in this situation is thinking about it.

"Yeah, I bet," I snap, rolling my eyes. "You must go through girls pretty fucking quick, since none of them want to come back for seconds."

Levi's eyes narrow, and he steps closer to me. Instinctively, I step back, ending up with my back against the wall between the desk and the bathroom door. He's got me boxed in, but I don't let him see that it bothers me.

When he drops his head, it brings his lips so close to kissing me, ghosting right over the skin of my cheek at the corner of my mouth, and I hold my breath, shivering a little when his fingers brush against my arm.

As much as I'm telling myself not to react, my body gives me away, and Levi chuckles under his breath, those deep brown eyes boring right into mine.

"Sure seems like *you* want seconds," he murmurs, and even the tone of his voice is enough to make me ache with something that feels suspiciously like yearning.

I don't let it set in though. Instead, I reach for the anger that's always close enough to the surface and use it to clear my head. I shove Levi's chest and step away from the wall, rolling my eyes and praying my face isn't as red as it feels like it is.

Fuck, I wish my body didn't want him. This would be so much fucking easier.

Levi just smirks and lets me move farther away. "Let me give you a tour," he says, dropping it for the moment. *Thank god.*

The rest of the house is big and well stocked, though I notice nothing is over the top or lavish. It's got everything three guys in their early twenties could possibly need. They each have their own rooms with attached bathrooms, and there's an extra bathroom for guests. The living room has a large, flat screen TV against one wall with every imaginable gaming console hooked up to it.

There's a large gym in what used to be an unfinished basement, Levi explains, and he shows me the equipment, including weights and machines and a few heavy bags hanging from the ceiling. I perk up a little at the sight of those. At least I can keep up with my training while I'm stuck here. That's something.

We head back upstairs and go into the kitchen. Even *I* have to admit it's beautiful. All the appliances are shiny and silver and new, a long way away from the beat up old oven and refrigerator in our kitchen back home that Dad found at a yard sale a few years ago and has been repairing diligently ever since.

Sloan and Rory are both in the kitchen when we enter, the former leaning against the counter while Rory rummages in the fridge. Sloan seems content to ignore me as Levi points out the toaster, the microwave, and the fancy coffee maker that you just have to put the little pods in.

"You want a drink, Mercy?" Rory asks, gesturing to the well-stocked bar cart in the corner. I never told any of these guys my name, and they never told me theirs, but I guess we're long past the point of official introductions.

"No," I say shortly. "I'm going to bed."

He looks at me for a second like he's giving me a

chance to change my mind. But even though a drink actually sounds really good right now, I don't.

After a moment, Rory shrugs, and I turn on my heel and head back up the stairs. None of them try to stop me, and I can hear the sound of them talking in the kitchen as I take the stairs two at a time to get back to my room and close the door behind me.

I undress and shower, washing the day off me, but it's not like it goes away. The suds swirl down the drain, and I dry off and pull on clothes to sleep in, but my mind is still going a mile a minute.

I'm worried about my dad. Worried about whatever it is that the Black Roses want him to do, and even more worried about what will happen if he can't do it.

I'm also super conscious of the three guys who are presumably still downstairs in the kitchen. Even with a whole floor between us, I can't get them out of my mind.

They've all gotten under my skin, albeit for very different reasons, and I find myself dreading having to face them in the morning—and for however many days after that until my dad pays off his debt.

Despite the longer shower, my thoughts haven't settled at all as I turn off the light and crawl into the unfamiliar bed.

The mattress is comfortable, and the pillows are plush, but no matter how long I toss and turn, I can't get to sleep.

5

I MUST HAVE DOZED off sometime in the early hours of the morning, because I wake up with the sun streaming into the room, sprawled out on the bed.

Clearly, I kicked the covers off at some point in the night because they're bunched at the foot of the bed, half hanging down to the floor.

I lie there for a second, letting the events of the night come back to me.

Fuck. It all really happened.

It's all real, and not some kind of messed up bad dream. It feels silly to admit, but a part of me definitely hoped that I would wake up back in my creaky old bed at Dad's house, and none of this would have happened. Like a nightmare fading away when you wake up and realize it's not something you have to deal with in real life.

No such luck.

I blink slowly, trying to will my hazy, half-asleep brain to come back online, when the reality of the situation asserts itself once more in the form of the bedroom door opening and Rory walking right into the room.

He stops in the doorway, and I can feel his gaze raking over me.

I'm just in a tank top and panties, the way I usually sleep, and he's getting a fucking eyeful.

Rory whistles, low and amused, and I spring out of bed, suddenly wide awake. My beat-up old suitcase is open right next to the bed. I reach for the first thing I can get my hands on, a shoe, and chuck it at him, going for another when he ducks the first, laughing.

"Get the fuck out!" I snap, and he obeys, still cackling like an idiot as he closes the door behind him.

Furious, I throw on clothes, barely paying attention to what I'm yanking on, and march down the stairs just a moment later.

All three of the guys are in the kitchen, drinking coffee and lounging against the counters like apex predators, and I stop in the doorway, hands balled into fists.

"What the fuck is wrong with you?" I demand. "Just because I'm stuck living with you, that doesn't mean I'm your fucking property. I knew the Black Roses were into some shit, but I didn't think you were *that* shady. Are you dealing in human trafficking now? Finding sex slaves or whatever-the-fuck that you can do whatever you want with?"

I'm breathing hard, eyes narrowed as fury courses through me, and Rory is still fucking laughing. Levi's eyebrows are in his hairline, and if I didn't know any better, I'd say he looks impressed with the force of my rant.

Sloan just looks pissed, but I haven't seen a different facial expression on him yet.

As if he can sense me thinking of him, the blond man pushes away from the counter, setting his cup down before stalking over to me and getting in my face. "You should consider yourself fucking lucky to be stuck *living* with us," he snaps, brow furrowed and steely gray eyes narrowed to match mine. It's impossible to miss the way he emphasizes the word *living*. "Shit could have turned out way worse for you and your father."

"What the hell is that supposed to mean?" I snap right back, rage making me reckless.

I know exactly what he means, but I don't want to admit it. I don't want him to think I'm intimidated by him for a second, even if he is taller and broader than me, like he's made of pure fucking muscle.

Instead of answering me, he just shakes his head, and I huff, my anger climbing. "My dad could fucking take you," I spit out. "*I* could fucking take you."

Sloan snorts, and it's a dismissive sound. "Trust me, princess, the only way you'd get me on my back is if I've got my cock inside you."

Before I get a chance to tell him to shove his cock up his own ass, he stalks past me out of the kitchen and disappears into the rest of the house, leaving me with Levi and Rory. My hands are balled up into fists, and my jaw is clenched so hard I swear I'm about to crack a fucking tooth.

Levi still isn't saying anything, but Rory holds up his hands. "I didn't mean to upset you, Your Highness," he says, in that same kind of half-joking, half-serious way he's been talking since I met him. He does a little bow that makes me want to kick him in the balls, but even *that* comes off as kind of charming, the asshole.

"Why were you in my room in the first place?" I press my lips together, folding my arms and glaring at him.

"I just came up to ask what kind of stuff you want for the kitchen," he answers. "Since you'll probably be here for a while, I figured I'd make sure you have some things you like. You know, snacks, coffee, tea, that sort of stuff?"

I open my mouth and then close it, taken aback by that explanation. He's actually trying to do something nice for me? What the hell?

It throws me off balance because I wasn't expecting it. Last night, I would have said for sure that they intended to make me eat whatever they wanted me to eat, holding over my head that I was lucky they hadn't killed me and my dad or whatever, basically like Sloan did just a few minutes ago.

But Rory's standing there looking honest and earnest, as if he *actually* wants to know what kind of food I'd like in the house. I'm not sure what to do with that, so I fall back on old habits and give him a flippant answer.

"Sure. Let me give you a list."

He gestures me to the white board that's stuck to one of the doors of the double sided fridge, and I take the marker and start to write whatever comes to mind. Random shit that I've seen in weird stores or heard about from watching cooking shows when nothing else is on.

Matcha, goat jerky, gochujang, finger limes, frogs legs, pickled peppers, spam, frozen calamari.

I add more random condiments and then step back to look at Rory, almost daring him to complain about the list.

He just laughs like he always does, his green eyes glittering. "You're so weird," he says, but he's grinning even as he speaks.

I don't like it. I especially don't like the way his expression warms a little as he looks at me.

Even with me throwing shit at him and giving him a hard time, he still looks at me like he wants to devour me, and I don't know how to deal with that.

I hate living here. I hate this whole situation.

I hate *him*.

It would be so much easier to do that if he hated me back.

6

LATER THAT DAY, I'm in my room with the door closed. I'd never admit that I'm hiding, but well... I'm kind of hiding.

I don't know what to do with these guys or how to act around them, so I figure it's better if I keep some distance between me and them until I can figure out a plan or something.

I dig around in the pocket of my jeans from last night and find my phone, pulling it out so I can text my dad and make sure he's okay. I should have done it earlier, but the stand-off in the kitchen distracted me. I'm also not entirely sure I'm allowed to be in contact with him while he does whatever "favor" the Black Roses are demanding of him. But no one has explicitly told me not to, so I figure I'll just do what I want to until someone tells me otherwise.

I fire off a quick text asking how he's doing and if there's anything I can do to help him, then sit cross legged on the bed, waiting for a reply. It comes back after a few minutes, short and to the point.

DAD: I'm fine. I'll get this done as fast as I can and get you out of there, but I'll probably be unreachable for a while. Love you, kiddo. I'm so fucking sorry.

My lips curl into a grimace as I read his message several times. I wish I could do more for him, but I'm glad to know he's still alive. The Black Roses have kept their word about that so far. It's something, at least.

Fuck, I wish I could hear Dad's voice and have him hug me and tell me everything's going to be all right. But since there's no way that's gonna happen, I do the next best thing and call Scarlett.

She answers on the second ring, her voice shockingly light and happy. "Hey! How's it going?"

She doesn't know any of what went down last night, so she has no idea how dramatically my life has changed in the past twenty-four hours. She probably thinks I'm calling to see if she wants to go get a burger or something.

I fucking wish.

"Not good." I don't bother sugar coating things or beating around the bush. We've known each other too long and have seen each other through too much bullshit for that. "I've got a story for you. Are you sitting down?"

"Oh, shit. Let me go to my room." I can hear her

moving through her apartment and then settling on her bed. "Okay, I'm sitting. Go."

I hesitate for just a second, not sure where to even start, but then I just start talking. Scarlett is my best friend. She's been there for me since I was a little kid, fresh off losing my mom and growing up with just my dad in the kind of neighborhood we lived in. She was right there with me for everything, and I never have to pretend with her.

So I let it all pour out. I start from the second she split last night, telling her about walking in to see my dad getting jumped by the Black Roses, and how the three guys she was so hot for were a part of it. I tell her about trying to stop them from hurting my dad, about being captured and taken to that gas station place, and about the ultimatum I'm now a part of.

"Basically, I'm a glorified prisoner," I tell her. "They've got me at their house, which is honestly probably one of the nicest places I've ever been in, but that's not the point. Until Dad finishes whatever deal he's made with them, I have to stay here, and it sucks."

"Oh my god." Scarlett mutters. "Holy shit. Oh my fucking god." I can hear the surprise and anger in her tone, and it feels good to know I'm not the only one who's outraged by the turn of events. "That's so shitty, Mercy. I mean... it could be worse, because gang members or not, those guys are fucking fine."

"Jesus, Scar, can you focus for like a second?" I flop back on the bed, rolling my eyes.

The worst part is... she's not wrong.

I can't fucking stand them, but that doesn't change the fact that they're three of the sexiest guys I've ever met. Even Sloan, pissy and irritable as he is, has an undeniable appeal to him, and just being in the same room as them is hard. Hence why I'm hiding away.

But I don't have time to daydream about dangerously gorgeous guys. I have a mission here—protect my dad and find vengeance for what they're doing to my family.

My father is all I have, all the family I've got left, and I'll be damned if I let them take him away from me.

"Sorry, babe." Scarlett sounds genuinely chagrined. "I shouldn't even be joking around about that shit right now. I'm just still trying to process all of this."

"Yeah. Me too. And you're right. They're fine as hell. I just can't let it blind me to what's beneath all that, you know?" I murmur. I don't want to scare Scarlett, but we've both lived in this city our whole lives, so she has to know how serious this is. "You know how the Black Roses are."

She sighs. "Yeah, we hear rumors about the stuff they get into all the time. Please be careful, Mercy, okay? I know you're doing this for your dad, but these fuckers are no joke."

"You don't have to tell me that." I snort, chewing on my lower lip. "And I can take care of myself."

"I know, hot stuff. And you know I've got your back no matter what happens."

I smile, feeling for the first time since I woke up this morning like some of my equilibrium is coming back. Scarlett has *always* had my back, and I've always had hers. If I need her, she'll come running. I miss my dad, but just hearing my best friend's voice is enough to make me feel better, and I gaze up at the ceiling with a little sigh, feeling some of the tension drain out of me.

I can hear Scarlett moving around on her own bed and then the sound of typing.

"What are you doing?" I ask.

"Research," she replies. "On your guys."

"They're not my anything," I insist.

"You know what I mean. Tell me their names again?"

I do, filling her in on the little I know about them, which is mainly what they look like and the fact that they're in the Black Roses. So nothing she doesn't already know.

I hear her typing frantically for a little bit and then she sucks her teeth, clearly annoyed. "There's not much available here on any of them."

"That's not surprising. It's not like they go around broadcasting the shit they do. They keep a low profile."

"There are some pictures here, though." She lets out a low whistle. "Goddamn, Mercy."

"Scar, please."

"I'm just saying! This Sloan guy? He looks like he stepped off the cover of GQ. That jawline, yum."

I roll my eyes, but once again, she's right. I made the same judgement when I first saw him myself. I flash back to how he looked when he was leaning over me, angry and in my space, and I can feel myself flushing again, heat moving through me slow and thick.

No, no, no. For fuck's sake, Mercy!

I shouldn't be fantasizing about any of them. Least of all Sloan, who looks like he would kill someone without a second thought.

"Rory's an interesting character," Scarlett continues, snapping me out of my thoughts.

"Rory's a pain in the ass," I mutter. "What did you find?"

"He's done some fighting before. Like your dad, but not as serious, it looks like. Sloan's apparently the son of the current leader of the Black Roses. Some guy named Gavin Kennedy. He's next in line to take over."

That makes sense. I remember the man who seemed to be in charge last night, and the resemblance between him and Sloan. Shit. That means the leader of the Black Roses himself is involved in whatever's going on with my dad. That can't be good.

So they're skilled, these assholes who I have to live with for the next... however long. Rory's built like a fighter, muscular and quick under all that teasing, so that makes sense, and Sloan's ruthless and probably good in a fight himself if he was raised by the leader of the Black Rose gang. They're hot and badass on top of it, the kind of men I definitely would go after if I saw them in a club or at a fight and didn't know who they were.

But I hate them anyway.

Because I *do* know who they are.

Nothing I hear from Scarlett changes the things they've done to my dad, and I have to stay focused on that.

"Thanks for looking into it," I tell Scarlett. "I'll just have to figure out more about them while I'm here."

I don't tell her about my plan to find out enough about the Black Roses to give myself some kind of bargaining chip if it comes down to that. I'm not sure it's a good idea to talk about that anywhere in this house, including my new bedroom. I highly doubt the room is bugged or anything like that, but it would be stupid to get complacent.

"Keep me posted," Scar replies. I can hear the worry in her voice. "And like I said, be careful."

"I will," I promise. "On both counts. Take care of yourself."

"Always, babe."

I feel better when we hang up. Bolstered by the extra bit of confidence, I finally creep out of my room. The house is quiet, and I wander around downstairs for a bit, poking around here and there. The living room is neater than I would've expected with three dudes in their twenties all sharing the space, and I peek at their collection of DVDs and games, not surprised to see it's all action movies and shooters.

Like they don't get enough violence in their real lives?

The couch is leather and plush as hell, but I resist the temptation to sit down on it. I don't want to be comfortable here, and I definitely don't want one of them to come in and see me making myself at home. With my luck, it'll be Rory, ready to make some stupid jokes about what he'd like to do on the couch with me, and the calm I've managed to hold on to will be shattered.

Bored with my exploration, I head back upstairs and follow the sound of music to a closed door that's a little way down the hall from my bedroom. I remember Levi pointing it out as Rory's room, and I smirk, getting an idea.

It's stupid.

Fucking with any of these guys is like playing with fire.

But clearly, he needs someone to show him what it feels like to be barged in on. If I'm going to be living with these three assholes for who-knows-how-long, they all need to learn to have a bit more respect for other people's personal space.

So, just like he did to my room earlier, I open the door wide and step inside.

And then I freeze, my eyes almost popping out of my head. The snarky comment I was about to make dies on my lips.

Standing in the middle of the room, fresh from the shower and wearing only a towel slung low around his waist, is Rory.

For a second, all I can do is gape at him. *Everything* is on display, from his damp golden brown hair to the thickness of his arms and the tattoos that wind their way up both arms, over his biceps and shoulders in two full sleeves.

I've got a half sleeve on my right arm, colorful swirls of ink that I saved up for months to get done. I can admit I've got an affinity for tattoos, and his are fucking stunning.

His pecs are well defined, just like his abs, and it all leads down to his hips and the cut lines at his hips that point like a damn arrow to his crotch, barely covered by the towel around his waist. A thin trail of brown hair forms a path leading right to what is probably a big ass dick if the rest of him is any indication.

My mouth literally waters before I can do anything to stop it, and I'm definitely frozen in place, staring like a fucking idiot.

Rory's surprised expression melts into a smug smirk in a matter of seconds, and he puts one hand on his hip, drawing my gaze right back down to his crotch again. Dammit.

"If you're starting a tit for tat, you better be prepared for the tat," he says, one eyebrow lifted and mischief sparkling in his bright green eyes.

"I can handle you any day of the week. You're really

not that impressive," I retort, not even sure what I'm saying as I slam the door closed and lean against it for a second, trying to catch my breath.

My heart is racing like I've just run a marathon, and my face is flushed as hell. *Again.*

Fuck. This is getting out of hand.

Just when I'm about to go back to my room and not come out for the rest of the day, Rory's voice startles me from the other side of the door. "I know you're still out there."

"Fuck you," I mutter and stalk off quickly, trying to put as much distance between myself and his door as humanly possible.

But even when I'm safely ensconced back in my room with *two* doors between us, it's not enough distance. It's nowhere near enough. I'm not sure any amount of space between me and Rory could erase the images of what I just saw from my mind's eye.

Well, that fucking backfired.

7

THE NEXT MORNING, I get up early. Maybe it's just because I'm awake before Rory is, but there aren't any surprise walk-ins, so I can consider that progress, at least. I get dressed and throw my books in my bag, thanking whatever higher power might be out there that it's Monday and I have a reason to get out of the house.

It's quiet when I go downstairs into the kitchen, and I breathe a sigh of relief, rummaging around in the cabinets and refrigerator until I come up with some nice bread to make toast with butter and jam.

Taking a chance, I perch on one of the stools at the little breakfast bar and eat my toast, washing it down with some juice, keeping an eye on the time as I munch away. If I'm lucky, maybe I can get out of here before any of the guys are up. And then maybe they'll all be gone when I get back, and I can avoid interacting with them for an entire day.

No such luck.

Less than a minute after I have that thought, Levi comes walking in, dressed and only a little bleary eyed. He makes a beeline straight for the coffee maker and pops one of the pods in.

"I'm going to be taking you to school." He shoots a glance over his shoulder at me, then turns to lean against the counter while he waits for the coffee to brew.

"No fucking way," I say immediately. "I don't need a babysitter."

It's confirmation that they're going to let me keep going to school though, which is something I was worrying about in the back of my mind. They could have just told me I had to drop out, dangling my dad's precarious situation over my head until I agreed.

My plan was to just sneak out anyway and see if they tried to stop me, but apparently that's not necessary because I'm going to have a goddamned escort.

"Look, I'm not thrilled about it either," Levi says with a sigh. "There are other things I could be doing. But it is what it is, so you're my baby for as long as this situation lasts, I guess."

I hate the sound of that, especially the way him calling me his *baby* makes my skin heat up. Motherfucker. I've been doing so well this morning up until now, not letting my thoughts run away from me, but just hearing him say that makes me flash back to the things he said to me when we fucked last year.

I shove the last of my toast in my mouth and drain my glass of juice in one gulp just to have something to distract me.

"Fine." I bite out the word, making it clear I'm not happy about it even if I don't have a choice. "We need to leave in five minutes."

That barely gives him enough time to finish letting his coffee pour into the cup and then transfer it into a travel mug, but I don't care. If I have to suffer, then so does he.

We get into the same car from when they abducted me, but this time I sit in the front passenger seat. I don't give him any directions, but once again, he doesn't need them. I don't like him and his goons knowing so much about me, but I keep my mouth closed for the moment.

"Not much to look at, is it?" he says when we get to the campus, glancing at me as he slows down to let a group of students pass across the street.

I scowl immediately, hackles up. I go to a community college on the south side of Fairview Heights, and it's more than fine. It's not like my dad had the money to send me to some fancy school, and I didn't have the grades to get scholarships and all that. I'm not ashamed of it, but Levi's comment gets under my skin.

"Where do *you* go to school?" I retort, turning my head

to give him a look. "Somewhere fancy? Some Ivy League university? Because if not, then maybe you should shut the fuck up."

He shakes his head. "I don't go to school. It wasn't in the cards for me. I've got other skills, another life path, you know. I'm fine without it."

Unless I'm imagining it, there's a slight sadness to his tone. Maybe something like regret, but it's hard to tell for sure. I can't get a good read on his expression as he keeps his gaze straight ahead and doesn't let go of the steering wheel.

Interesting. Did he want to go to college? Did he have dreams of getting a degree and then going on to make something of himself?

I know that's all my dad wants for me. For me to have a better, *easier* life than he had. For opportunities to come my way, and for me to take them and make the most of my life.

But there's no real way I can ask Levi about his hopes and dreams for the future. It would be too fucking personal, and besides, I don't want him to know I'm curious about him at all.

Honestly, I don't even think I can picture him sitting in a classroom, taking notes or asking questions like some kind of average student. There's nothing *average* about any of these guys. So I just ignore his comment and file the information away for later.

He flashes me a cocky smile just a second later, glancing over and winking in my direction. "Besides, I don't need college. I've got plenty of skills. You can attest to that, can't you?"

I roll my eyes, letting the innuendo and the moment pass.

Once he parks the car, we get out and walk across campus. My first class is a good hike away from the parking lot, and I'm not looking forward to walking with Levi for the whole thing. It's pretty clear he's not just going to drop me off and leave, or wait in the car for me to be done for the day.

Before we get halfway there, I hear someone shout my name. I don't even have to look to know who it is, and a second later, Scarlett comes hurtling up and gives me a hug so tight I can feel my ribs protesting.

"You're here!" she says, squeezing me.

"I'm here," I echo, wheezing a little. "Scar, you're killing me. Lemme go."

She's still grinning when she steps back, but then her eyes dart to Levi and her brows shoot up into her hairline.

I watch as she sizes him up, and while he's taller than her by a good bit, I can tell when she decides she can take him. Her hands go to her hips in a trademark pose I know well. It's the stance she takes when she's about to rip someone a new asshole, but I cut in before she can make a scene.

"Scarlett. Not now."

"But—"

She looks at me, and I shake my head quick. Her lips turn down in a pout, and I know I've ruined some of her fun. She loves when she has a chance to verbally destroy someone, and it's not like Levi doesn't deserve it, but I'm already running late for class, and I don't want to deal with this here.

Besides, with my dad still indebted to the Black Roses, I have to be careful how far I push my luck with these guys. Rory just seems entertained when I sass him, and Levi seems pretty unflappable, but Sloan already seems to hate me. The last thing I need is to push any of them too far and get myself or Dad into more trouble.

"Let's just go," I say and start walking off, leaving the two of them no choice but to follow me.

We head the rest of the way across campus, and Scarlett seems content to ignore Levi, acting like he's not even there as she chatters about campus gossip and a new hairstyle she wants to try. It's purposefully boring and over-the-top girly, not the usual kind of shit we talk about at all. She's probably doing it to annoy Levi, even though he doesn't say anything about it or seem bothered by it at all.

When I glance at him, he's looking around the campus, hands shoved into his pockets. Interestingly enough, he doesn't stand out as much as I would have thought he would.

He's tall and quiet, but there are plenty of tall and quiet guys around. Someone whizzes by on a skateboard, a bright pink hat barely containing blonde curls, and it's perfectly normal. Maybe he would have been able to blend in if he'd gone to college. Maybe it's just my perception of him that makes that whole concept seem weird as hell.

"Okay, I should go," Scarlett says, breaking into my thoughts and jerking her head in the direction of the science building. "I have to go pretend like I understood the chem homework."

I bite back a grin, because I know she probably does understand it a lot better than she thinks. She holds herself to a super high standard and is never satisfied with anything but perfection, which is why her grades were a lot better than mine in high school.

"Have a good day, Scar."

"You too," she says, pulling me in for a quick hug before giving Levi a look that clearly says *I've got my eye on you.*

I watch as she walks off, then turn to head toward the humanities building in front of us. "I have two classes in there," I tell Levi.

"Okay," he replies. "I'll be out here." It sounds more like a threat than a promise when he says it.

"Super," I mutter under my breath and then head in.

Nothing in my course schedule for this semester is that rigorous that it requires my constant focus. I'm mostly doing my Gen Ed requirements, sitting through basic English Lit classes and a math class that I'm pretty sure I already took in high school. It's a good stepping stone toward getting my degree one day, once I've figured out what I want to do with my life.

Thinking about that makes me think about Dad, and how he's always said I could do anything I put my mind to. He wanted more for me than just fighting and living at home with him, but it's hard to think of a future when you're not sure what you want from it. It's even harder now, when I can't think about the future without thinking about what could happen to him.

I already lost my mom. I can't lose my dad too.

Professor Kennings drones on up at the head of the class, talking about symbolism in Pride and Prejudice, and I barely hear what he's talking about, doodling in the margins of my notebook and staring out the window.

When we're finally released, I throw everything back in my bag and peek outside to see that Levi is still there, posted up outside the building with a look on his face that keeps anyone from getting too close.

Jesus. Apparently the Black Roses are serious about keeping an eye on me. Levi's positioned so if I even thought about leaving the building to run off somewhere, I'd have to go right past him. Unless I climbed out of a window or something. Most people don't have the kind of time on their hands necessary to stand there while someone else is in class, but I guess this counts as Levi's job now. Babysitting me full-time.

I roll my eyes and head to my next class.

That one drags on with just as much boredom as the first, and I pay even less attention. The three guys I'm now living with are going to be bad for my grades if this keeps up, but it's hard to focus with everything going on.

Finally, I'm freed for lunch, and I follow the stream of students out of the building and into the sunshine. Levi is in the same spot, looking at something on his phone, but he glances up and meets my gaze as I get close.

"What's next?" he asks.

"Lunch. I'm starving."

"Good. *Someone* didn't let me get breakfast this morning."

I roll my eyes and start walking again, trusting him to follow. Sure enough, he falls into step with me just a second later. "I'm sorry, but it's not my fault you didn't get up with enough time to eat before stalking me across my campus. That's on you."

He doesn't argue, and I just keep walking.

After a bit, I glance at him again. "You know, this is a lot of fucking effort to go to, just for one man and his daughter. We're nobodies, and you're making it seem like we're important or something."

He glances at me but doesn't answer. There's a flicker of something in his eyes that makes me pause though.

It makes me feel like maybe I'm wrong. Maybe there's something else going on, and I'm more important to the Black Roses than I know.

Or, more likely, my dad is.

It's clear Levi isn't going to say anything else about it, and I don't bring it up again, instead keeping the thought tucked away in the back of my mind to explore later when I have more information.

The Fairview Heights Community College campus is in a busy enough neighborhood that there are plenty of restaurants and food trucks within walking distance. Most students head for the popular chains, ready to grab burgers and fries or overpriced salads before they have to go back to sitting in the hard chairs and listening to professors who want to be there about as much as we do.

But I figured out a while ago that those fast food joints are only worth going to if you're desperate and in a huge hurry. I'm neither of those things today, so instead of heading toward any of those places, I lead Levi over to one of the food trucks that's parked just about a quarter mile away from campus.

It's one of those that looks kind of shitty from the outside, dingy and mud-splattered from driving in the rain. There's a grinning pig painted on one side, and the paint is peeling a bit in spots and faded in other places.

It's not much to look at, and I can see Levi's skepticism as we walk up. Of course. Someone like him who lives in that big ass house and probably eats whatever expensive take-out he wants wouldn't know anything about the joy of a greasy sandwich from a shitty food truck in the middle of the day.

It's one of the city's best kept secrets, and I guess if he's going to be tailing me for the whole damn day and into the future, then he's going to learn about it, because I'm not letting these assholes deprive me of good food along with everything else.

I grin at the man in the window, who's used to seeing me by now, I'm sure. "Two steak sandwiches and fries, please," I tell him.

Before I can fish my wallet out of my bag, Levi is passing over a credit card, and I roll my eyes but don't argue.

"A gentleman!" the owner says, grinning and swiping the card before handing it back to Levi. "Ten minutes."

I nearly strain my eyes trying not to roll them. If this guy only fucking knew what Levi's real deal is, I doubt *gentleman* would be anywhere in the top ten descriptors he might use for my companion.

Oblivious to my thoughts, the food truck owner turns back to the griddle behind him and gets to work. A second later, the air is filled with the sounds and smells of sizzling meat and peppers.

My stomach growls, and Levi snorts under his breath, but I ignore him until we're presented with two large sandwiches wrapped in foil, nestled in plastic baskets next to a pile of fries.

There are a few picnic style tables just down the hill in a little park area, so we go to sit there, each taking a side. I unwrap my sandwich and bite into it, making a happy noise as I chew the spicy steak and peppers and then attack the fries.

When I look up, Levi is watching me instead of eating, and I make a face at him. "What? It's getting cold."

He just shakes his head, but I can see a smile pulling at his lips.

Whatever. Girls eat. And not all of them eat like ladies.

It's... more comfortable than I would have expected it to be, sitting here eating with him. We chew our food in silence for the first several minutes, but it's not tense or awkward.

It gives me the push I need to speak up and do some digging. Despite what Rory said last night about me maybe living with them for a while, I have no idea how quickly my dad might manage to accomplish the task they gave him. And as much as I hope it's soon, I need to take advantage of every minute I have with these guys to learn more about them and their organization.

"The Black Roses are a pretty established gang, huh?" I ask through a mouthful of fries.

Levi nods. "Well enough, I guess. They've been

around since I was little. Been running the city for years, fending off the Jackals for almost as long."

"How long have you been a member?"

He glances away for a second and then down at his sandwich, and I half expect him not to answer me. But after a second, he does.

"Years. At first, I was just on the fringes, I guess. Doing random jobs if they wanted me to, mostly on the outside looking in. My brother was a member, so that was kind of my in."

"He *was*?" I speak around a mouthful of steak and peppers. "Like, past tense? Did he quit? I didn't think that was allowed."

"It's not," he replies. "He died. Six years ago. I became a full member after that."

I stop chewing, my jaw freezing in mid-bite.

Oh. Huh.

Somehow I haven't thought about the three men as people who have close family connections. I mean, the leader of the Black Roses is Sloan's father, but I'm willing to bet they don't have the close relationship that I have with my dad.

But when Levi speaks, his voice is the careful kind of neutral that means there's pain there when he talks about his brother.

It makes me feel bad for him, and I want to kick myself

for even thinking that. I don't want to see the human side of these guys at all.

They're the villains.

The bad guys.

The ones who swooped in and took me away from my Dad and are now holding me hostage.

If I start thinking of them as real people with emotions and thoughts and feelings about things other than being shitty, it's going to get weird fast.

"I'm sorry," I say anyway, mostly because I have to say something. You can't just hear that someone's brother died and say nothing. I want to ask how it happened. If it was an accident, or if there was some kind of fight or gang-related attack or something. But I don't.

Still, Levi must see the sympathy in my expression before I can totally shove it down. He reaches out and touches my arm, his dark brown eyes softening as he looks at me.

"It's okay. It was a long time ago," he says quietly.

It's an innocent enough gesture, but the touch of his fingers on my arm is electric, sending sparks flying and racing up my spine. I barely bite back a sharp inhale, pressing my lips closed and trying to keep my posture casual and relaxed.

Jesus. I don't know what it is about this guy that makes me react this way whenever he touches me. I can't help but remember the time we hooked up. It was a year ago, but

Levi's even more built and sexier than he was then. I couldn't resist him back then, and it's even harder to keep myself from being drawn in by him now.

The air between us seems thicker, somehow. Our eye contact is charged, and I know he's thinking similar thoughts. There's no way it's just me that's feeling this, and if I wanted to, I could reach across the table and—

And nothing. No. *Bad.*

I give myself a mental slap and pull my arm away from Levi, taking a deep breath. He's not just some random hot guy who I can drag into the nearest empty room on campus and fuck. He's a member of the Black Roses, a high ranking one apparently, and he and his friends fucked my Dad over and nearly beat the shit out of him.

He's not someone to lust over. He's someone to hate and try to take down so I can keep my family safe.

That thought douses the fire that's trying to build inside of me like a splash of ice water. My jaw tightens, all the heat draining from my limbs.

We finish the rest of our lunch in silence, and it's probably for the best.

8

ON TUESDAY MORNING, Levi drives me to school again. I notice as we're sliding into his car that my bike is parked off to one side of the garage, and my eyebrows rise a little. He said something about having someone stop by to get it from Dad's house, but I didn't really think he'd follow through on that.

I also don't quite get why he bothered to have it brought over when it seems like the guys don't plan on letting me go anywhere unattended.

Either way, I'm grateful to see it here, although there's no way I'd go so far as to thank him or either of his two friends. Having my bike delivered is a nice gesture, but one nice gesture doesn't negate the fact that these men are holding me as a glorified hostage.

When we reach the community college, Levi escorts me around campus just like he did yesterday. Part of me hopes he'll get busted for loitering if he seriously plans on doing this every day, but I doubt there's much chance of that. He blends in too well with the other students. Even though *I* know he doesn't belong here, there's nothing about the way he looks that would make an outside observer suspicious of him.

We eat lunch together again, and we end up talking because sitting in silence is too damn awkward. He's surprisingly easy to talk to. He doesn't have the same easygoing flirtatiousness of Rory, but he's not as stoic and closed off as Sloan either. He's somewhere in between the two, friendly when he wants to be and quiet the rest of the time.

Honestly, it's his moments of quiet that draw me in more than they should—that feeling that there's more to him than meets the eye, parts of himself he doesn't share with most people. Even his brother's death is something I don't think he talks about much, and I get the feeling it means something that he told me.

After we get back in the late afternoon, I spend some time up in my room, half-heartedly poring over homework. It's not really like me to get ahead on studying. I tend to be more the type who's motivated by last-minute panic, so I do a lot of cramming and writing papers at zero hour. But right now, I'll do anything to keep my mind occupied and help pass the time.

Around eight o'clock, my stomach starts growling

aggressively, and I flip my textbook closed and climb off the bed.

When we got back to the house yesterday, there were grocery bags on the breakfast bar, filled with the random assortment of things that I asked Rory to get. On the counter in front of them was a note that read: *Enjoy, princess.*

I rolled my eyes so hard I swear I strained something. He had to know I was just fucking with him by asking for all that random crap, but of course he bought it anyway, fucking with me right back.

He came into the kitchen later that evening while I was poking around for something to make and grinned when he saw me with my head in the fridge.

"What culinary delights are you going to whip up tonight?" he asked, amusement lacing his tone. "I have to admit, I'm interested to see what you're planning to make with all those things you had me buy. I didn't take you for having such an eclectic palate."

I gritted my teeth and fought back the urge to tell him to go fuck himself. He was toying with me, clearly, his bright grin never slipping. But there was something like a challenge in his eyes too. If I admitted I wasn't going to eat any of it, it would've given him the upper hand to call me ungrateful or call my bluff, and there was no way I was going to give him the fucking satisfaction.

"I haven't decided yet," I replied airily, pulling the

gochujang from the fridge and debating before grabbing some chicken to go with it. "I'll work it out."

His smile didn't waver even a little. "Oh good. I'd hate for it all to go to waste."

His grin was so irritating, just like *him*, as he stood there watching me stumble through making something that resembled a stir fry with some of the ingredients he'd picked up.

In the end, it didn't actually turn out too bad. It was *edible*, anyway, which was all I was going for. There was a satisfied look on Rory's face as he watched me load up my plate. When I offered him some, he just laughed and headed out of the kitchen.

Fucker.

Tonight, there's no way I'm going to attempt to use any of the other random ingredients he bought for me, but I do need to eat something. I peek out the bedroom door to make sure the coast is clear and then pad downstairs to the kitchen. It's empty, thank fuck, and I pull open the fridge and then the freezer, searching for something quick and easy.

This whole situation is so fucking weird. It's like living with roommates, except knowing that your roommates could *kill* you if you steal their food or don't do your dishes.

I huff a quiet laugh at that thought. It's not really funny—none of this is funny—but if I don't laugh at it, I'll cry. And I've never been a big crier.

As I'm digging out a frozen pizza from the top shelf, I hear the front door open and close. A second later, Rory and Levi's voices filter through the house. I hesitate with the freezer door open, listening intently.

"...those fuckers down a peg," Levi is saying.

"Yeah, but that was easier when we knew what rules they were playing by."

Levi grunts in a response to Rory's words. They pass by the kitchen on their way to the stairs, and I realize they both must've been out taking care of some Black Rose business or other. They're dressed in dark clothing, and they both look more serious than usual. When they catch sight of me standing in front of the open freezer door, Levi lifts his chin in greeting.

He turns and heads toward the stairs, but Rory lingers, walking into the kitchen instead of following his friend. His green eyes dance with amusement as he settles onto a stool at the bar, cocking his head at me.

"Nice of you to defrost our freezer for us. It really isn't necessary though."

"Fuck." I grab the pizza and close the door, stopping cold air from wafting into my face. Then I waggle the pizza box at Rory. "Can I have this?"

"Sure. What's ours is yours."

I snort. "Somehow, I doubt that's true."

He grins. "It's not. But it seemed like the polite thing to say. And you *can* have the pizza."

Walking over to the stove to turn it on, I look back over my shoulder at him. "Where were you?"

He arches a brow, leaning one elbow back on the bar. "You know I can't tell you that."

"Right." I press my lips together. "No fraternizing with the prisoner."

Rory chuckles, a low, deep sound. "I wouldn't go that far. But no, I can't tell you Black Roses business, obviously."

There's a finality to his voice that makes me certain that no matter how flirtatious and laidback he is, he takes his loyalty to the gang seriously. But even though he's shut that line of conversation down, he doesn't leave. He just watches me pull the frozen pizza out of the box, his gaze tracking my movements with the lazy focus of a predator relaxing in the sun.

"Can I help you with something?" I finally ask when I can't take his silent attention anymore. My skin is prickling with awareness, and I'd like to pretend there isn't heat blooming beneath it, but it's hard to deny.

"Nah." Rory shakes his head, one side of his mouth tilting up. "It's just weird having someone else staying here. We've all gotten into our routines, gotten comfortable living together over the past few years, and now the house feels... different."

I slide the pizza into the oven, then close the door and

lean against it, crossing my arms. "You mean you haven't kept prisoners here before?"

He rolls his eyes. "You're not really a prisoner."

"I'm not?" There's a harsh edge to my voice. A challenge. "Really?"

He straightens a little, the muscles of his arms flexing as he pushes away from the bar. "No. If you were a prisoner, you'd know it. You're here of your own free will, aren't you?"

Irritation simmers in my veins. "If you call being forced to stay here as collateral until my dad pays off his debt a *choice*, then sure."

There's something in his expression I can't quite pinpoint, and he holds my gaze as he nods. "I *do* call it a choice."

He steps away from the bar, moving a little closer to me as the smell of pepperoni and melting cheese begins to fill the room.

"You didn't have to come with us, Mercy. You didn't have to cover for your dad's fuckup. It was *his* fuckup. His decision to screw us over. He had to know when he decided not to throw the fight that he was painting a target on his back, and on the backs of anyone close to him. But he did it anyway. You were there in the crowd that night. You saw it just like the rest of us did. He was *down*. It was *over*. He gave a convincing as fuck performance, putting up a good show before letting Guzman turn the tables on him. He didn't *have* to get back up. He chose to."

I swallow, memories of the fight flashing through my mind. It all plays out so differently in my memory now that I know Dad was supposed to go down and stay down. That he was supposed to lose.

What was it that made him change his mind? Was it just pride?

Why the hell did he do it?

My stomach clenches, and I glare at Rory. "Yeah? And you think I *shouldn't* have volunteered to come with you guys? That I shouldn't have done whatever I could to protect my dad?"

He holds up a hand. "I didn't say that. I'm pretty fucking impressed you agreed so quickly, honestly. Not everyone would do that. You're fierce as fuck. Brave too. It takes a certain kind of person to risk everything for someone they love." His eyes harden a little, something almost like anger tightening his expression. "I'm just not sure what kind of father puts his daughter in the position of having to make that choice."

I tighten my jaw. I don't like him talking shit about my dad, no matter what he did. That's between the two of us, and Rory shouldn't get to judge my Dad's worth as a parent.

"What does Gavin want him to do?" I ask, my voice thick. In his short, cryptic text, Dad didn't mention anything about what kind of task the leader of the Black Roses assigned to him.

Rory grimaces, looking almost regretful as he shakes his head. "Sorry, princess. I'd love to tell you, but that falls under the whole 'can't discuss Black Rose business' thing. Sloan is the one in charge here, and he answers to Gavin. It's not up to me what we tell you."

The fact that he actually sounds like he *would* tell me if he could doesn't make his answer any better. It only makes it worse. Because it reminds me that no matter how normal moments like this might seem, standing in the kitchen and talking while a pizza cooks in the oven, none of this is anywhere near normal.

Regardless of what Rory says, I *am* a prisoner.

I turn away from him, yanking open the oven door to check on the pizza as I try to get a handle on my emotions and control my features. I don't want him to see the disappointment on my face.

But either I turn around too slow, or Rory doesn't need to see my face to know what I'm feeling. I hear the sound of quiet footsteps as he moves a little closer, and when he speaks, his voice is soft and quiet. The usual flirtatious tone is gone, replaced by simple honesty.

"I'm sorry, Mercy. I might not respect your dad for putting you in this position, but I sure as fuck respect you. I meant everything I said, and whether or not you believe it, *not* everyone would've made the choice you did. That's why I tried to get some food and shit that you'd like in the house. I don't want you to feel like a prisoner. You don't deserve to pay for your dad's mistakes."

I don't answer. I just close the oven on the half-cooked pizza and stare down at the sleek, dark surface of the stovetop. There's a long beat of silence as Rory stands behind me, and then he makes a quiet noise in his throat and heads for the door. I wait for him to leave before glancing over my shoulder at where he was just standing.

He doesn't want me to feel like a prisoner, he said.

And the crazy thing is, in some ways, I *don't*. Having free run of the house, being able to use the kitchen whenever I want, and being allowed to go to school? All of those things help preserve some sense of normalcy in my life, making it almost possible for me to pretend these men are just three very pushy, dominant roommates I've been saddled with.

But forgetting I'm a prisoner might be more dangerous than being constantly reminded that's what I am.

Because if I lose sight of who and what these men truly are, I'll end up paying for it.

I just know it.

9

The next two days pass in pretty much the same way as the first two. I get up, go to my classes, and Levi's there all the damn time. We get lunch together, and then he follows me back to campus to wait outside while I finish up for the day.

Then we go back to the house.

Rory and Sloan are usually there by the time we return in the late afternoon. I have no idea what they do all day while Levi and I are out. Probably ruin other people's lives or something.

One nice thing about being stuck living with these men—as if anything is really "nice" about it—is being able to take advantage of the opportunity to try to find out what the hell the deal was with Dad's fight. Since they refuse to tell me, I've decided I'll have to dig up the answers on my own.

Like Rory said, the guys are all comfortable in their home, not used to having a fourth person around. That also means they're not used to having to hide anything, and I use that to my advantage. Sloan in particular has a lot of serious-sounding phone conversations, and I manage to find a place on the stairs that's hidden from the living room below but provides a good place to eavesdrop whenever someone is talking in there.

I manage to catch enough of a few conversations to piece together that there's something going on with the Jackals, the other gang that competes with the Black Roses for control of the city. Their rivalry is almost legendary, and most people fear being caught in the middle of it.

It all seems to point to something bigger going on that I don't fully understand, and I can only hope that whatever the hell is up, it isn't going to put my dad in more danger.

Other than going to class every day, I'm basically stuck at the guys' house. I wander between my room and the kitchen, trying not to linger too long in any one spot out in the open. Rory never misses a chance to tease me in a way that makes me both annoyed and flustered, and Sloan seems content to pretend I don't exist, only pausing to glare at me when he's in a bad mood.

Which is basically all the time.

I wish I could do the same and pretend they aren't there, but between Levi following me diligently every day and the way I can't ignore the other two, I'm sort of losing my mind.

They're not the only ones who aren't used to sharing space like this. I've been living with my dad while I go to school to save money, and suddenly being under the same roof as three guys in their early twenties is... an adjustment, to say the least.

They're all so fucking masculine, walking around all sweaty from time spent in the gym in the basement, or coming down from showers in sweatpants and thin shirts that leave nothing to the imagination. It's distracting and frustrating on multiple levels.

In an attempt to get some distance and keep myself busy after Levi and I return from school on Thursday, I grab a few tools and a rag from the garage and head outside to where my bike is parked. I've already put in dozens of hours and as much money as I could afford to get it running smoothly, but there are still more tweaks to be done.

Late afternoon sunlight warms my skin as I work, and I pause every once in a while to wipe my forehead with the back of my arm. I'll never be a pro mechanic, but I've learned enough from my dad and a couple of his buddies in our neighborhood to know what I'm doing.

I'm so lost in my task that I almost jump when the rumbling sound of a car approaches. Sloan pulls up in the driveway and cuts the engine, staring out at me through the window.

His gaze practically burns a hole in my skin, but I ignore him as he slides out of the car and slams the driver's side door shut. He's about to head toward the house when something Rory said the other night flashes through my mind.

Sloan makes the decisions around here.

He answers to Gavin, but he's the closest one to the top living in this house.

Before I can talk myself out of it, I repeat the question I asked Rory. "Hey. What is my dad doing for you guys?"

None of my eavesdropping has yielded an answer so far, and I want to know. I need to understand what's happening here, especially if I want to have a real chance of helping Dad as more than just *collateral*.

Sloan stops. Then he glances down at me where I'm crouched near the back wheel of my bike, his gray eyes narrowing slightly. "Am I the last one on your list?"

I frown. "What?"

"I know you already asked Rory about this. Did you ask Levi too? Am I the last one?"

A flush rises to my cheeks. Shit. I guess eavesdropping can go both ways. Was he listening in on my conversation with Rory the other night? Or did Rory tell him about it later? I don't know which option is worse, honestly.

Instead of answering Sloan, I lift one shoulder in a shrug, standing up and wiping my hands on the rag before tossing it on the ground.

"Is it a crime for me to want to know what's going on with my dad? Why won't you just tell me?" I gesture around at the house and the yard, where there's not another soul in sight. "Who am I gonna tell? The only people I talk to anymore are you guys and Scarlett, and I'm not gonna tell her anything that could put her in danger."

Sloan stares at me for a long moment. He's done such a good job of ignoring me for the past several days that having his entire focus turned on me so intensely now makes me feel like I'm under a microscope. I feel like he can see much more than most people do when they look at me, and I don't like it.

Silence hangs in the air between us, and he hesitates for so long that I almost start to wonder if he's actually considering telling me.

Then he shakes his head sharply, his eyes darkening. "I won't *tell* you because I don't *trust* you. You're your father's daughter."

His words piss me off. It's not that I really expect any of these men to trust me, and I certainly don't trust them. But I hate the way he's looking at me with his lip curling up in something almost like a sneer, as if I'm a piece of shit he wants to scrape off his shoe.

As if I'm nothing, and so is my dad.

I take a step toward him, my hands curling unconsciously into fists. "Yeah. I fucking *am* my father's daughter. And I'm proud of that. At least he works an honest living. At least his entire livelihood doesn't depend on wrecking other people's lives. He's a better man than you or any of your friends could ever hope to be."

Sloan snorts. "Tell yourself whatever you need to so you can sleep at night, sweetheart."

I grit my teeth. "Jesus, why are you such a fucking asshole? At least Levi and Rory make some attempt to not be dicks about this whole thing, but you seem like you're *enjoying* it. Do you get off on this kind of thing? On wrecking people's lives?" I let out a harsh laugh. "I guess you're your father's son too. I only met the guy once, and I can already tell he's an asshole."

Sloan moves fast, crossing the short distance that separates us and getting in my face. My adrenaline spikes, but I don't give any ground, not even as he looms over me.

Shit. That was stupid. It was definitely the dumbest thing I've done since I arrived here. Scarlett warned me to be careful, and insulting the head of the Black Rose gang in front of his son is the literal definition of the word "reckless."

But I don't care. Sloan doesn't get to talk shit about my dad like that. He doesn't get to pretend he's better than me or my family just because he has more power and sway in this town.

Fuck that.

"I would be *very* careful about what you say next," he tells me quietly, his voice a dangerous purr.

"Or what?"

Okay, I was wrong before. *That* was the stupidest thing I've done since arriving. I basically just dared Sloan to take out all the pent-up anger that always seems to simmer beneath his skin on me. I just threw down a gauntlet, openly taunting him.

His jaw tightens, and I can feel the tension in his body radiating into me from where his chest brushes lightly against mine. My own body tenses, ready to slip into fight mode and defend myself if need be. If Rory and Levi come outside, I'll be outnumbered, but if it's just me and Sloan...

Even if I don't win that fight, I could at least make him sorry he started it.

But Sloan doesn't make a move. He just stares down at me, his eyes bouncing between mine.

"You should stop asking questions about shit you don't understand, princess," he murmurs gruffly. "Levi and Rory can do whatever the fuck they want, but I'm not interested in making your stay here more pleasant. You're not here to be our friend. You're not here to be our *anything*. And we don't owe you shit."

With that, he steps back from me. The movement is slow, almost as if he's dragging himself away—or maybe it's just because the air is so thick with tension that it's literally become hard to walk through.

He turns and heads toward the house, stopping only to toss a few parting words over his shoulder.

"I *am* my father's son. And I'm proud of it."

With that, he disappears inside.

10

I STARE AFTER SLOAN, my heart pounding hard and fast. A dozen different emotions are crashing around in my chest, and I have to consciously work to uncurl my fingers from the tight fists they're wrapped in.

Part of me is relieved he left it at that, but another part of me—the reckless, stupid part—wants him to come back out here so I can punch him in his fucking face. I know it's dangerous to taunt any of the men who have become my keepers until my dad works off his debt, especially the boss man's son. But it's never been in my nature to sit down quietly and put up with assholes.

And Sloan is most definitely an asshole.

The sun is going down, the sky turning from orange to purplish-blue, and I grab the tools and the rag and toss them back in the garage. Sloan is nowhere to be seen as I head upstairs, but my body is still buzzing with adrenaline from our encounter.

Since I can't take out my frustration on his face, I decide to work off some of the stress by going down to their home gym.

I throw on a sports bra and some sweatpants and toss my hair up into a messy bun before heading back downstairs again, luckily not running into anyone on the way.

In the gym, I wrap my hands and do a couple of stretches, shaking the tension from my body before going over to one of the heavy bags and sizing it up.

It's bigger than the one I'm used to, but that's not a problem, and I give it a firm punch to start, warming myself up. It's been a little while since I've trained, so I start slow, feeling the burn start in my arms as I hit the bag over and over again.

It feels fucking good, especially after so long spent doing nothing, and once I feel like I've got a good rhythm going, I go full tilt, waling on the bag with hard punches, working my aggression and boredom out with each hit I land.

My breathing is hard, and I can feel sweat beading on my brow, but that feels good too. I've always been a physical person, more likely to work out my feelings with my body than with words. Some people like to talk about their problems, but I've never had to deal with anything I couldn't work out by going hard in the gym for a few hours and then taking a hot shower to ease the ache away.

I'll probably be a little sore tomorrow morning as my body adjusts to being put through a hard workout again, but it'll be worth it if it helps me clear my head.

I'm blind and deaf to anything but my hands, the bag, the sound of my harsh breathing, and the *thud-thud-thud* of my fists impacting the bag again and again, so when a voice breaks into my trance-like state, it takes me completely by surprise.

"You've got good form. A little stiff around the shoulders though."

I curse as I nearly have a heart attack, whirling around to see Rory standing near the door with his arms folded.

I'm panting like I ran a marathon, and I can feel sweat running down my back as I stare at him. He just stares right back, a little smile playing at his lips.

He's dressed in just a wife beater and gym shorts, so he clearly came down to work out himself, and I have to suck in a breath at the way he looks. Once again, his tatted arms are on display, the full sleeves winding up over his shoulders and down to his wrists. With his arms folded, his biceps bulge, and I remember that Scarlett told me he fights sometimes.

It's clear in his build that he's good at it, and fuck, that's hot.

My mouth feels dry, and my heart is still racing, but I try to chalk that up to the exercise, not his appearance.

Realizing I've probably been staring at him for longer than can be blamed on surprise, I scowl a little. After the encounter I just had with Sloan, I probably shouldn't be talking to any of these guys, but Rory started it this time.

"I don't need your tips," I say. "I'm doing fine without them."

Rory shrugs and then walks over to the wall where the equipment is kept. He grabs a pair of pads and slips them onto his hands before coming over to the open center of the room and taking a defensive posture.

"Show me what you've got then, princess."

His tone is teasing, but I can tell he's serious. Something about his blasé attitude and the nickname riles me up, and my competitive nature takes over, which is kind of a relief since it works as a distraction from taking in how goddamned hot he is.

I'll take whatever I can get at this point.

"Fine." I purse my lips, accepting his challenge and striding over to square off with him.

He's bigger than me by a lot, but I've been training with my dad for years, which means I've fought a lot of guys. I take down bigger opponents all the time. I roll my neck and shift into a better stance and then lash out, hitting the pads with the same force and rhythm that I was using on the bag.

Rory takes each hit, eyes intent as he braces himself, letting me go for a bit before he smirks and then swipes out with one arm, making me duck under the blow.

"Keep your weight balanced better so you can avoid a punch after throwing your own," he tells me.

I make a face, but I have to admit it's actually a useful note. But I'll be damned if I ever say those words out loud, so I just nod, letting out a breath and moving back into position.

My focus narrows again, and Rory keeps up with me easily, blocking each hit and forcing me to stay on my toes. He trades off between giving me blows to dodge and making me move around, getting my footwork into it as well.

I'm breathing hard, sweat dripping down my temples, and he seems cool as a fucking cucumber, calling out teasing quips as we continue.

"Ooh, there was some fire in that one," he says when I land a particularly hard punch.

"I was imagining it was your face," I snap back, and he laughs and pushes me back a bit.

"Aw, you're going to hurt my feelings," he teases. "Here I am trying to be helpful, and you're thinking about hitting me." He cocks a brow. "But between you and me, I don't think punching would be the first thing you'd want to do with my face."

I glare at him and lash out harder, but he blocks each hit easily.

"Think whatever you want," I grunt. "Doesn't change the truth."

He's a good fighter, I have to give him that. He's not as polished as someone who does it all the time, like my dad, but he's got really good instincts and natural balance and a sort of grace that carries over from the easygoing way he is in life, I guess.

He makes each block look effortless, and I have to work hard to take him by surprise. It's a good thing for my training, and I have to grudgingly admit that I'm enjoying myself.

Of course, there comes a point when he gets too cocky. He's laughing, dancing back a bit and making me come to him, holding his hands up higher so I have to reach up to hit them.

"What would you do if you had to fight a guy so much taller than you?" he taunts, eyes bright with amusement.

I'm not even short, and his constant joking is grating enough that I decide to take him down a peg.

"I'd aim for his balls," I reply. Then, instead of kicking him right in the dick like I'd really like to, I drop a little and sweep his leg out from under him, sending him sprawling to the floor in a heap. I go down with him in a smooth motion, taking advantage of his vulnerable position and straddling him in a full mount.

He looks surprised at the takedown but not upset about it, and I spare a second to wonder what it takes to really get under this guy's skin.

"Whoa, Hurricane. That move definitely isn't regulation." He chuckles, grinning crookedly.

"So? I fight dirty. What're you gonna do about it?" I shoot back, staring him right in the face, daring him to make a big deal about getting his ass kicked by a girl.

His grin grows, and he bucks his hips, shifting his weight so he can flip us over in one fluid motion that leaves me surprised and breathless, flat on my back. I end up pinned under him, one of his legs between mine, his face just inches away as he holds himself up above me.

"I do everything dirty," he says, his voice dipping down into a lower tone that pulls a shiver up my spine.

He's close enough that I can smell him, sweat mixed with something fresh and clean under it. And I can feel him against me, hot and getting hard, either from the sparring or the proximity or both.

Shit. This was a bad idea.

I'm still emotionally on edge from my fight with Sloan and everything else that's happened over the past week. A restless sort of energy is creeping under my skin, and it has to get out some way.

It needs some sort of fucking release.

I lick my lips, feeling my own body responding to his obvious arousal. My nipples are hard, pressing against the thin material of my sports bra, and there's a throbbing ache between my legs. It's a struggle not to push up and rub against the sturdy thigh that's wedged between mine, but I'm trying to keep my distance, trying to ignore the thrumming, pulsing heat inside me that's calling me to grind against him and give in to the pleasure I want to feel.

Rory's eyes widen a little. His gaze lingers on my face for a second before it drops down to my mouth, and I don't know which of us moves first, but the thread of tension that's been growing this whole time finally snaps.

We're kissing a second later, his mouth hard and hot against mine, demanding and unyielding. I arch up with a soft gasp into his mouth, hands going to his shoulders, holding on to him like I need an anchor.

Whatever I'm hoping to save myself from by clinging to him, it doesn't work. The searing heat between us just grows, and Rory laughs under his breath, pressing me harder against the floor as he slips his tongue into my mouth.

I definitely don't mind the tongue, or the aggressive moves. No one's ever accused me of being passive when it comes to shit like this. I'm not some soft girl who needs to be wooed and coddled, and I prove that by shifting under him until I have enough leverage to roll us over once more, feeling triumphant when I end up on top of him.

Of course Rory kisses like he does everything else, playful and teasing, but with a hard edge to it. He licks into my mouth, coaxing my tongue to tangle and slide with his, and then runs his hands down my back to land at my hips. They rest there for a second, and he drags me in closer, letting me feel how hard he is as we kiss.

I can hear myself moaning into his mouth, and if I were in my right fucking mind right now, I'd tell myself to shut up. To not let him know that he's getting under my skin. To not let him hear how much I like this.

But I'm very much *not* in my right mind, so all I do is press down harder, rubbing against him and enjoying the hard slide of our bodies together before he flips us one more time, reclaiming the top spot.

It's almost like sparring, the way we keep shifting the upper hand, mouths clashing together. There's nothing timid or gentle about it, and that makes it even better. Even harder to resist.

Rory chuckles into my mouth and bites down on my lower lip, and that sends a jolt of pleasure through me so strong that it's enough to snap me out of the haze I've been in. I blink my eyes open and push at his chest, breaking the kiss.

"Get off me," I manage, and I hate how raspy my voice sounds.

He smirks but does it, pushing off of me and getting to his feet easily. He holds a hand out for me to take, but I ignore it, rolling to my feet without his help.

We're both flushed, chests heaving as we fight for air,

and it's not from the sparring. Looking down, I can see the hard line of Rory's cock through his gym shorts, and I know my nipples are probably still very visible in my sports bra.

True to form, the fucker is still grinning. His hair is tousled, and it's clear he enjoyed himself.

"I'll spar with you any time, Hurricane," he says, and I fight the urge to punch him.

"You should be so lucky."

I bite the words out, and I've barely finished speaking before I step around him to head for the door. I have to get out of there. Just the smell of him, still so close, is enough to make me want to lean back in and pick up where we left off, but it would be a fucking mistake. That's not what I'm here for.

That's the *opposite* of what I'm here for.

As I pass him, he reaches out and slaps my ass, the sound echoing around us. It's not a hard slap, but it's hard enough. The small sting of pain is followed by a flush of warmth that seems to melt my lower belly into a molten pool.

My jaw clenches as I shove down every emotion inside me but the anger. I flip him off over my shoulder and let the door close behind me, pausing for just a second to take a deep breath.

Shit. Where the hell did that come from?

It's one thing to spar with the guy, but I should never have let it turn into anything else.

In some ways, it's not hard to see why it did though. Fighting and sex are two of my favorite things, especially when they're combined, and it's not hard to imagine Rory being good at both. His cocky confidence is well-earned, even if it is a pain in the ass to deal with.

Literally.

11

ALL DAY FRIDAY, I have a harder time than usual focusing in class.

To be honest, it's the same distraction I spent the rest of last night dealing with, replaying the make-out session with Rory over and over again in my head until I can't think about anything else.

I remember the hard lines of his body against mine, and even the way he moved when we were sparring. His form. His stance. The way he moved in time with me to block my punches and keep me on my toes, almost like we were dancing together.

Half of it is how skilled he is, and being impressed with him for that, but the rest is all me being wrapped up in my horribly ill-advised attraction to him.

Even after a long, mostly cold shower last night, I wasn't able to shake the mental images floating around in my head. I crawled into bed and was one second away from giving in to the need that was riding me, making me wet between my legs. It would have been so easy to slip a couple of fingers into my pussy and rub at my clit with the other hand so I could get myself off to thoughts of what might have happened if I hadn't come to my senses on the gym floor.

But I held out somehow, reminding myself over and over again that I couldn't give in to the temptation.

So what if they're sexy as fuck? They're also assholes, and that matters more than anything else.

There are a million sexy guys out there, and when this is all said and done, I can go find one of them to work off some of the frustration settling under my skin from living with these guys.

Of course, when I came down this morning to make myself some toast and coffee, Rory was already in the kitchen, making his own cup of coffee in the French press and winking at me when he saw me. It was pretty clear from his expression that he'd been thinking about what we did too, and it was only the fact that Sloan called him into the living room that saved me from whatever teasing shit he probably wanted to say.

But the damage was already done. I spent the whole ride to campus with Levi staring out the window, wondering what Rory's dick looks like.

Fuck.

At least Sloan has gone back to ignoring me, pretending our encounter outside the house never even happened.

I can only hope my dad is able to do whatever it is he has to do to fulfill his part of this bargain soon, because I'm losing my fucking mind living with these guys.

It's hard for me to keep my head on straight around them. But I need to focus up if I'm going to accomplish what I set out to do before my dad comes back and gets me out of this hellish living arrangement.

There's definitely something up with the Black Rose gang. Something more than the usual shit they get up to, I mean. Sloan's refusal to talk about it yesterday only makes me more certain that I'm right.

I want to know what it is and how my dad fits into it, and more than that, I need to get something I can use against them to keep them from fucking with me or Dad ever again.

Professor Kennings drones on and on up at the front of the room, talking about symbolism and character growth or something like that, and it's easy to let myself daydream instead. Usually, I'm more attentive in class than this. I at least *try* to be anyway, but today I really can't help it.

Instead of English literature, my thoughts are back at the house, jumping back and forth between memories of my confrontation with Sloan and rolling around on the floor with Rory.

"Ms. DeLeon?"

I nearly jump when I hear my name and finally come back to focus to see the professor looking right at me, one eyebrow raised expectantly.

The rest of the class is silent and watching, half of them looking at me, and half of them watching Kennings. I get the feeling he's asked me a question that I definitely did not hear, and he's waiting for an answer.

"Well?" he adds. "I'm sure you have some input here."

For a second I stare at him, trying to remember anything about what he was just talking about so I can put together some kind of answer, but it's mostly a blank. The last thing I can remember him saying was something about the countryside, but I can't actually tell how long ago that was. The lecture could have moved on to anything by this point, and unless he's been lecturing about the way Rory's collar bones look in a tank top, I've got nothing.

There's a hiss from my left, and I glance over to see one of the guys in the class looking at me. He smiles and then leans in a little, the fact that we're close to the back of the room hiding the motion.

"Heathcliff," he whispers to me, then grins.

Sure, okay. It's not like I have anything to lose, and I'm willing to bet that saying *something* is better than staring like an idiot and saying nothing at all.

"Heathcliff," I repeat, raising my voice a little.

Professor Kennings narrows his eyes at me, looking like

he's been deprived of a moment of joy. But instead of saying anything or calling me out again, he just nods and moves on, talking about how sometimes the villain in a story will be represented by the atmosphere or the setting.

As Kennings goes back to rambling and pacing at the front of the room, I breathe a sigh of relief and shoot the guy next to me a grateful look. Now that I'm not panicking about being put on the spot, I recognize him. His name is Dean Something-or-Other, I think, and he has at least one other class with me. He's tall, with dark hair and blue eyes, and the sort of build that makes me think he played sports in high school.

But that's basically all I know about him. We've never really talked, but there's a sort of camaraderie that comes from us both sitting near the back for the few weeks we've been in this class.

Dean smiles back and mouths "no problem," before going back to his notes while Kennings drones on.

Annoying as it is to be called out like that, it definitely takes me away from the thoughts I don't want to be having in the first place. Luckily, the class ends soon after that, giving me a break from the stifling air of the classroom and the chance to get up and move around to clear my head. As usual at the end of class, we all stream out of the building and into the sunshine. I'm glancing around to see where Levi's lurking when I hear someone call my name behind me.

Dean strolls up, smiling, slinging a bag over his shoulder. He looks even better out of the washed out light of the classroom, and I can't help but smile back.

"Kennings is a dick sometimes, huh?" he asks.

"Oh yeah, definitely. He hasn't called on me for the whole semester, but the one time I'm not paying attention, he decides to put me on the spot in front of the whole class." I shake my head and smile back.

"I think he gets off on it sometimes," Dean says. "He looked so disappointed when he didn't get to shame you in front of everyone."

I make a face at that. "I really don't want to think about what gets Kennings off, actually."

The man has a face like a toad, and the attitude to match. I'd almost rather go back to thinking about Rory than think about my professor getting any kind of gratification up there in front of us. *Almost.*

"Thanks for the save though," I add. "I would have made an idiot of myself without you."

"My pleasure." Dean shrugs, giving a little nod. "You seemed like you were thinking about things a lot more important than Wuthering Heights."

You have no idea.

Ugh. I will myself not to blush. The last thing I need is for this guy to ask me what I was thinking about, because there's no socially acceptable way to explain that my head was full of thoughts about fucking one of the men who's basically keeping me hostage, and I don't have a convenient lie in place just yet.

Instead, I just force a little laugh and smile at him. "Yeah, that's not hard to do. If this class wasn't a requirement for Gen Ed, I'd have dropped it in a heartbeat."

Dean nods and shifts closer to me as another group of students move past us. "I don't blame you. It's boring, and I'm pretty sure I read all these books in high school already. Hated them then, so I'm not sure why they expect me to give a shit now."

"And now we have the honor of paying for it." I make a face. "Lucky us."

He laughs. It's a nice sound. Warm and open, and the way he smiles makes his eyes even brighter. "So, hey," he says, changing the subject abruptly. "I know we don't really talk or anything, but you seem pretty cool, so was wondering if maybe you'd like to get lunch or something—"

Before he can finish his sentence, an arm drapes itself over my shoulder.

I tense in surprise. I'm ready to knock the arm away and read whoever it is the riot act for daring to come up and touch me, but then I turn my head to see Levi standing there.

He leans into me possessively, eyes narrowed as he looks Dean over. Then he smiles all of a sudden, looking flirtatious and happy when he turns back to meet my gaze.

"Hey, babe," he says in that low tone that makes me

want to punch him in the dick and then kiss him senseless. It's not even remotely close to being fair.

I just stand there, surprised and not sure what the fuck he's thinking, and then he ups the ante by dropping a kiss to my cheek and looking right back at Dean like he's daring him to finish the sentence he started earlier.

"Oh," Dean mutters. "Sorry. I didn't know."

He looks as surprised as I feel and more than a little put out, but he—wisely—doesn't say anything, instead just giving me a tight smile and then going on his way.

I wait until he's gone and we're mostly alone before I round on Levi, jerking out of his hold and wiping at my cheek like I can get rid of the feeling of his lips there. It's more for show than anything, because I can still feel the lingering warmth, and I know my cheeks are pink. I hate, absolutely hate, how easily these men affect me.

"What the *fuck* was that?" I demand, jaw clenching as I glare at him.

He just shrugs, looking like he's not sorry and doesn't care one way or another if I'm pissed off about it.

"What were you gonna do, Mercy? Go out with some guy while you're under our watch? Gavin's been pretty damn lenient about this whole thing, letting you stay in school while your dad pays off his debt. But there's no fucking way any of us are going to babysit you on a date, and there's no way you're going on a date without one of us there. See how the math doesn't add up? I was doing you a favor."

"A *favor?*" I repeat, incredulous. "I don't know if anyone's ever explained the definition of the word 'favor' to you assholes, but you clearly don't get what it means. Holding someone hostage doesn't count as doing them a favor."

Instead of responding to that, he just glances after Dean, narrowing his eyes. "You seriously wanted to go out with that pretty boy?"

No. Not really. But...

"That's not the point!" I glower at him. "The point is, my body is my own. Who I fuck or date or what the hell ever is nobody's business but mine. It sure as hell doesn't concern you or Rory or Sloan. I don't know why I have to keep saying this, but just because I have to live with you *temporarily* doesn't mean you own me. I can do what I want."

Levi... doesn't seem convinced. There's a look in his eyes that seems to suggest he thinks it's very much his business, and he should have some say. It's a little possessive, a little hungry, and a little too full of over-the-top male pride for me to deal with for another fucking second.

I roll my eyes and march away, ready to be done with this asshole and his bullshit, but just like I knew he would, he follows me anyway. Of course. Because he's my goddamn babysitter. I *have* to deal with him until the day is over, and then I can go back to the house and slam a door in his face.

The worst part of it is that I know he's not wrong.

He might not've acknowledged my words about being their hostage, but that's still what I am. Just because I get to leave the house sometimes and they're not keeping me locked up or chained to the bed or something, it doesn't change the stark reality that I'm faced with.

While I'm staying with them, they have some level of power over me. Just because they choose not to exercise the full extent of it often doesn't change the fact that I'm in a precarious situation.

As long as I'm under their roof, I can't live the way I want to. Not without their say-so.

I clench my jaw, refusing to let my gaze drift over to Levi where he walks by my side.

Please, Dad. Hurry up and do whatever they asked you to.

I still need more time with these guys if I want to gather damaging information about the Black Roses, but at this point, I'm not sure I even care about that anymore.

I just want out.

12

"Fuck, Scar. I don't know how much longer I can deal with this." I let out a plaintive groan, lying flat on my back on my bed. "It's like being in fucking prison. All week, I've got Levi on my ass, following me around, making sure I can't do anything fun, and then when I'm here, I have to deal with all three of them. I go to class, I come back, and I hide from them in my room—because if I don't, I'm likely to punch one or all of them in the face at any given moment."

It's been another exhausting week, and I'm pretty close to losing my mind. After Levi's stunt with Dean after my class last Friday, I've been giving him the cold shoulder, but it hasn't done anything to change the fact that he's still always *there*.

Usually, on the weekends I have plenty to do. I go dancing with Scarlett or go to a fight. I go to the gym, do grocery shopping, whatever. Something other than sitting in a room, staring at the same four walls.

I could go downstairs and make use of the guys' gaming systems or watch a movie or something, but the tradeoff of having to deal with them doesn't seem all that worth it.

"The worst part is, I still haven't heard from Dad. I feel like anxiety is eating me alive." I shake my head, letting out a breath. "I don't know if it would be better or worse if I knew what he's supposed to be doing for them, but at least if I knew *something*, maybe I wouldn't worry about him so damn much."

"Yeah." I can practically hear the grimace in her voice. "That sucks. He's strong though. He's a fighter. You know he'll be okay."

I nod, chewing hard on my lower lip. I know the first two things are true, and I try to let my faith in my dad's strength convince me that he'll come out of this just fine. But it's hard. He's just one guy, and I have no idea if what they asked of him was reasonable or not.

What if it's some Herculean task that *no one* could accomplish? What if that's why they gave it to him? As a way of just fucking with him, punishing him for not throwing the fight like they asked?

My mind starts spiraling through dire thoughts and imagined scenarios again, and I drag a hand through my hair.

"Fuck. I need to get out and get some space or I'm going to go crazy." I sigh.

"So go out," Scarlett says. "What's the worst they can do?"

"I don't know, lock me in my room? We haven't really talked about the boundaries of this... arrangement. Except that I can't go on a date without one of them chaperoning me, which none of them will do. So basically, I can't date."

She sucks her teeth, making an annoyed sound. "They sound like control freaks."

"They really are," I agree immediately. "I mean, I told you what happened with Dean last week. They act like just because I have to be here with them for the foreseeable future, they can run my life. I'm fucking sick of it."

"Maybe it's time to test the waters a bit," Scarlett suggests. "They can't really expect you to just sit at home doing nothing, right? You're a young, hot woman in the prime of her life. Making you into a boring old homebody is a crime."

I laugh at her outraged tone and roll onto my stomach. "Something tells me it's not a crime they really care about. But you're right. I need to see what they'll let me get away with. Clearly I can't go out with a guy without them getting all alpha male on me, but maybe getting a drink with a girl is okay."

"Yes!" She perks up immediately at that suggestion.

"You should come out with me. We'll get drinks and go dancing or whatever. Have a girl's night!"

It feels like it's been forever since I've seen my best friend for more than five minutes at a time on campus, so the idea makes me smile. It sounds like the perfect thing to get me out of the funk I'm in and give me a little space to clear my head from the guys. Not that I think they'll let me go alone, but in a club with the dim lights and ever shifting crowd, it should be pretty easy to get some distance.

Sitting up, I square my shoulders. "Okay. I'll tell them and then text you."

"Yay, I can't wait! Let me know what they say."

I hang up the call and leave my room, padding downstairs. My three keepers are in the living room, Rory and Levi on the couch while Sloan is draped over the armchair. There's a movie on the TV, but they don't seem to be paying too much attention to it.

Rory is the first one to see me when I walk in, and he pats the spot on the couch next to him with a grin. Levi glances over at me and then back to the TV, and Sloan seems happy enough to pretend I'm not there at all. That's fine with me.

"I'm going out," I announce, arms folded.

Levi lifts an eyebrow and hits pause on the movie. "Is that so?"

"Yes. It's so. I've been nowhere but class and this house since you brought me here, and you can't keep me locked up forever. I'm not trying to run away or whatever. I just need a break. You can come if you want, but I'm going."

None of their expressions have changed one bit. I grit my teeth, determination rising up in me.

"Look, I don't know why my dad didn't throw that fight. Fuck, I don't know why he agreed to throw it in the first place. He's always fought fair, and he's never let anyone buy him before." I pause, wrestling my emotions under control. "But he's trying to make amends for that now, right? He's playing along, doing what you guys are asking of him. So am I. I'm not gonna run or do anything shady. I just need to get out for a little while before I go fucking nuts." I hesitate again, and the last word is the hardest one of all. "Please."

The three of them exchange glances, and Sloan goes so far as to shrug. "Fine. It's not like we had anything to do anyway."

"Let's all go," Rory suggests. "I could use a night out. It's been a while."

Honestly, I'm shocked that I got my way. I truly expected them to tell me to fuck off back to my room and maybe lock the door on me for good measure, but I'm not about to complain.

I'm also not about to thank them, so instead I just tell them we're leaving at eight. Then I dash upstairs to shower and change into a short, curve-hugging dress after I text Scarlett to let her know.

For the first time since they abducted me, we all pile into the car. Rory takes shotgun this time, leaving me in the back with Levi while Sloan drives. Rory chatters the way Rory always seems to, and the other two respond, leaving me alone for a change.

I tell them the name of the club, and it's no surprise that they already know how to get there. They know the city inside and out, it seems.

Sapphire is one of those clubs that gets especially packed on a Friday night. It's close enough to both the community college and the main university that college students can get there by bus or car to blow off steam after a long week. The drink specials and the fact that the DJ isn't terrible make it a popular spot, and the place is already loud and chaotic when we get there and manage to find a place to park.

Scarlett's waiting outside once we walk up, and she throws her arms around me as soon as she sees me. She looks good in a tight red dress, low cut enough that it shows a good bit of her cleavage, with a hem that barely hides the tops of her thighs. She's wearing matching heels that lift her to being just an inch or so taller than me, and she takes advantage of it to see over my shoulder when she squeezes me tight and starts eyeing up the guys.

I just roll my eyes, but have to admit they do look super hot.

I've never seen them dressed nicely before, since

usually they're in jeans and t-shirts or gym clothes when they're around the house. But they all put in some effort to go out, even though they really didn't have to. Honestly, all three of them could have shown up in paper sacks, and they still probably would have been the best looking men in the place.

Rory's shirt is tight enough to show off his pecs, and the sleeves are short, so his tattoos are on display. His hair is artfully tousled, making it look like he might have just rolled out of bed and come to dance, which of course is designed to make people think about him in bed. The asshole.

Levi's dressed casually as usual, though his jeans are a bit tighter than ones I've seen before, and the sleeves of his long-sleeved shirt are rolled up, showing off strong forearms. His natural hotness is enough to make the outfit look better than it would have on anyone else, and there are already people eyeing him as they walk past us into the club.

Of the three of them, Sloan seems the least pleased to be out, even though he's dressed the nicest. His button-down shirt almost matches the color of his storm cloud eyes, and the sleeves are rolled up like Levi's. His jeans are dark, unsurprisingly. I don't think I've ever seen him wear a bright color before. It doesn't really matter since monochrome works for him, and his male model status is untouched.

Scarlett's eyes look like they're nearly falling out of her head as she looks them over, and I grab her arm and drag her inside. I already know the three of them are probably the most gorgeous guys present, and unfortunately, so do they. We definitely don't need Scarlett drooling over them to drive the point home.

The point of going out tonight is to cut loose a bit and think about something other than the three of them and how frustrating they are. To stop worrying about my dad nonstop and get out of my head a little. In fact, I resolve that until we leave, I'm not going to think about my three keepers at all. Instead, I'm going to do my damnedest to enjoy myself.

I nod with determination, and we split up from there. The guys head for the bar, and Scarlett and I watch as they order drinks from the obviously interested bartender. None of them seem to give her the time of day though, and they take their drinks and move to stand at the perimeter of the large space, avoiding the main section of the club where people are dancing.

They stand together, serious-faced as they talk, and for a second, I consider trying to eavesdrop on their conversation. It's probably Black Rose business, and it could be important, but with the music and the crush of people, there's no way I'd be able to hear anything anyway. So maybe, for tonight, I'll just forget about it.

I deserve a break, after all, and there's no telling when the next time I get to come out will be.

Scarlett still has a hold on my hand, and I let her lead me over to the bar. She has to practically lean all the way over it to flag down the bartender, but manages to put our drink orders in, voice raised to be heard above the thumping music.

I bob my head while we wait, already feeling the tension from the week starting to bleed out of me. With the guys out of sight and the prospect of a night of dancing and cutting loose ahead of me, my mood is better than it's been since all of this started.

Scarlett plasters herself to my side, already working her hips in time to the music.

"God, I can't believe you get to live with those three," she says, her gaze finding them where they're leaning against the wall, giving off clear "fuck off and don't bother us" vibes while they talk.

"You say that like it's some kind of prize." I snort. "I don't *get* to live with them. I *have* to. I don't have a choice. And I don't want to talk about them tonight, okay? I just want to blow off some steam."

She leans over and presses a messy kiss to my cheek and then squeezes my shoulder as two shots are pushed our way by the bartender. "You got it, hot stuff."

When she pulls back, her blue eyes are serious. I know she can tell how fucked up I am about all of this, and she can probably see how badly I need to get out of my own head. She puts on a wide grin as she picks up both shot glasses and hands one to me. "Bottoms up!"

I follow her lead and knock back the shot, feeling the burn of the tequila as it blazes its way down my throat. In just a matter of seconds, the warmth of it fills me, and I feel myself getting more relaxed. Thank goodness for Scarlett and her fake ID, not that this place makes a habit of carding.

"Okay," Scarlett says, setting her glass down on the polished wood of the bar and putting her hands on her hips. "Dancing. Let's do this."

I laugh, and we make our way to the dance floor, weaving through the throngs of people with the same idea. There's not much space that isn't already occupied by other bodies, gyrating and grinding to the low, sensuous beats, but we manage to find a little section to claim for ourselves and just go for it.

Dancing is always fun for me. It's almost as physical as fighting, and there's something so freeing about shutting my brain off and just letting the rhythm take over. Scarlett and I have done this at least a couple times a month since we were old enough to get into places like this, and we dance together for a few songs, arms overhead and hips swaying to the beat.

The crowd grows and shrinks and moves around us as people come to join or leave occasionally to flood the bar between songs. In the gaps between people, I can just make out the sight of Levi, Rory, and Sloan, standing in the same spot and looking like they're having an absolutely terrible time.

None of them are smiling, and Sloan looks particularly surly, but I don't care. It's my first night of freedom, the first time I've felt truly free since this whole mess started, and I'm not going to let his continuing bad mood ruin my night.

I turn so that my back is to them and start working it to the next song that comes on, a remix of a song that was popular half a decade ago. It's old, but it gets the crowd hyped all the same.

Scarlett's dancing in front of me, her eyes closed and a smile on her face. When a guy slides into a free spot behind her and starts dancing with her, she just goes with it, grinding back on him and dropping it low to the beat of the song. I laugh, glad to see her enjoying herself, and even happier to be here with her. I keep dancing, letting the beat take over, my body moving to the rhythm.

A few seconds later, I can feel someone moving in behind me, pressing themselves close to my back and then a little closer. I turn my head to see a guy, taller than me with sandy blond hair and dark eyes. He grins, and I smile back before turning around again and pressing back into him more.

There's a low chuckle that I can just barely hear over

the music, and he puts his hands on my waist so he can drag me even further back. I match my movements to his, grinding on him, swaying my ass and letting the slow, thumping beat of the song set the pace.

It's easy like this, just to lose myself in it. Not worrying about anything, just out with my best friend, feeling the beat of the song and the adrenaline of having a good time working through me.

I think about getting another drink once the song is over, or finding another partner to dance with, and it's almost like things are back to the way they were before all this shit started. They aren't, but it's much easier to pretend when I don't have Sloan and his cronies in my face or climbing up my ass about what I want to do.

I catch Scarlett's eye, and she gives me an exaggerated wink and a thumbs up. I shake my head but laugh anyway.

There's a second where the song is about to change, the beat of the new one fading in over the beat of the old one, and I push my hair back out of my face, feeling the sweat from being packed in with so many other people beading on my brow.

Before the next song can even play, I hear a sudden yelp and a curse from the guy behind me. I barely have time to look over my shoulder into the suddenly vacated space before I'm being lifted up and slung over a strong, broad shoulder.

For a second, I'm too stunned to do anything, and I

look down, trying to figure out who the fuck has their hands on me. I recognize the back of the shirt and the pants as the outfit Sloan was wearing.

Of fucking course.

"Let me go," I snarl. But it's mostly lost as the song picks up steam, the thumping beat blaring through the space.

With long, heavy strides, Sloan starts carrying me out of the club, and I'm left with the sight of Scarlett staring at me, open mouthed.

She's not the only one either. Everyone who was dancing around us is looking, wide eyed, and I can feel humiliation burning through me, hot on the heels of the ever-present annoyance that these guys make me feel.

We're outside almost before I've processed what's happening. The air outside is like a slap in the face after the close heat of being packed in with so many other bodies, but my face is still flushed with embarrassment and anger.

Raising my arm, I bring my elbow down hard against Sloan's side, right above his kidney. He grunts in pain, his body tensing up instinctively against the blow.

I elbow him again, and he sets me down hard. The second I'm on my feet, I lunge for him, trying to get my knee between his legs so I can slam it right into his balls. He twists, avoiding the strike, and holds me at arm's length, gray eyes snapping with fury.

"We're not here to be your personal fucking body-guards when you attract low-lives by grinding on their junk on the dance floor," he practically spits.

I narrow my eyes at him, arms folded. He's being a jerk, but that's nothing new. He's been a jerk since the moment I met him. What *is* new is the possessive look in his eyes and the way he's being so damn over-protective. What does he care if I grind with a stranger in the club? It's none of his fucking business.

"Fuck off," I shoot back. "You told me we could go out tonight, and I'll dance with whoever the fuck I want. You don't like it? Don't watch."

I turn to go back into the club, but Rory grabs me around the waist and starts towing me back to the car. He pins my arms by my sides in a move that reminds me of the first night I met him, when he dragged me away from the locker room where I was trying to protect my dad.

I didn't even see him or Levi step outside with us. But they're both here, of course. These three are like each other's shadows, constantly together, always backing each other up.

"Come on, Hurricane," Rory grunts.

I struggle against his hold, but that just reminds me that he's the only one of these three who's actually a trained fighter. He dodges my attempt at a headbutt again, and as the few people who are gathered outside the club turn to look at us, I have to weigh how much of a fight I want to make this.

If I get the cops called on these guys or something, I doubt that'll go well for my dad. Or me.

We end up in the back seat as usual, and Rory pulls me right down into his lap. Now that no one can see us, I resume my struggles, fighting his hold. The last thing I want is to be held right now, but he's not letting go.

I think about elbowing him right in the chest, but even as I consider it, I realize that he's not upset at all about my struggling. Far from it, judging from the hardness I can feel under my ass. It's just like when we were sparring, and he pressed that long, hard length against me.

My face is hot, but it's not just from being pissed anymore, and I feel a flash of arousal burn through me, right alongside my anger and embarrassment. I can count on one hand the number of times I've been manhandled this way, but it's becoming too much of a trend with these fucking assholes.

As much as I hate it, I have to admit there's something hot about the way they can just pick me up and put me where they want me to be. It turns me on, and I fight the urge to clench my legs together and feed the fire that's trying to spread.

Levi starts the car, and as we pull away from the curb, I take that opportunity to crawl out of Rory's lap, breaking his hold finally as he relaxes his grip. He's still grinning, and I try my best to ignore him, pulling out my phone so I can text Scarlett and let her know what happened.

There's already a message from her waiting for me, and I sigh softly when I read it.

SCAR: Holy shit!!! R u okay????

ME: Fine. The guys are just being dicks. Not allowed to dance now, apparently.

SCAR: Ugh, fuck them. We were having fun! And who just carries someone out of a club like that??

Her next text is just a bunch of angry emojis that almost make me smile. Before I can type anything back, the little bubble that indicates Scarlett is still typing pops up, so I wait.

SCAR: You should have seen their faces tho. Rory and Levi were behind Sloan, and they all looked jealous as hell. Sloan looked like he was about to kill someone as soon as that guy put his hands on you.

I blink in surprise as I read her message. I can definitely believe that Sloan looked like he wanted to kill that guy because he always kind of looks like he wants to murder someone, but the other two being jealous? For what? They didn't want to dance with me. They just want me to be miserable and bored, apparently.

ME: I think they were just pissed off that I made them come out.

SCAR: You didn't see it. There was definitely jealousy there. I'm telling you!

I quickly turn my phone over on my lap so none of the guys can see my screen or the texts, then angle my body and stare out the window, brow furrowed.

There's no way Scarlett is right. She must be reading too much into it and thinking there's something there when it's not. I can't believe they would be jealous just because some random dude was grinding on me.

They don't even like me.

There's no fucking way.

13

THE DRIVE back home feels like it takes fucking forever.

And the longer I think about what happened at the club, the more pissed off I get. Every time I try to do something for myself, something to have fun and try to forget about how shitty things are, one of them comes in and fucks it up. They act like they have the right to dictate what I can do and who I can do it with, and for what?

Because they think I'm going to run? Because they don't trust me? Probably all of that and a big dash of disrespect thrown in too.

They treat me like some kind of child half the time and try to ignore me the other half, except for Rory, who likes to alternate between treating me like a child and treating me like a future hookup. The point is, they don't treat me like someone with wants and thoughts and feelings of her own. They act like I need them to intervene on my behalf, even though I've been living my life perfectly fine for years before they came crashing into it.

I threw myself at their mercy to save my dad, agreeing to live with the three of them for an indefinite amount of time with no questions asked. I haven't objected once to being followed around every time I go to class. I've never made it seem like I'm a flight risk, and they still don't have enough common sense to realize I'm not going anywhere.

Where would I even go? They own most of the city, and there are Black Rose members all over the damn place. How would I escape them? And why would I abandon my dad? He's all I have, and there's no way in hell I would risk it.

We finally pull up back at the house, and I'm out of the car before any of them can say anything. I stomp inside once Sloan's unlocked the door, fully intending to go up to my room and barricade myself inside for the rest of the weekend so I don't have to deal with this bullshit.

Levi stops me before I can even get to the stairs. "What's your problem?" he asks, arms folded and one eyebrow arched as he cuts off my escape route.

I stare at him, shocked that he would even ask me something like that after what just happened.

"Oh, I don't know, Levi," I snap, the anger I've been feeling since Sloan grabbed me coming through in my voice. "Maybe it was being dragged out of the club when I just wanted to have a night out with my best friend? I'm sorry, being dragged would have been more dignified, actually. I was thrown over Sloan's shoulder like a fucking sack of potatoes in front of everyone and then hauled out like I'm some kind of naughty child when all I wanted was to blow off a little steam!"

"You were—"

"I don't want to hear it." I cut him off, raising a hand. "I already got it from Sloan about how you're not my bodyguards. Make it my fault, whatever."

Levi just sighs, but Rory grins, as per fucking usual. "If you want to blow off steam so bad, we can take you out," he says.

I narrow my eyes at him. Even in the face of my anger, they're all so fucking confident and bossy. They ruin my plans and then come up with their own, and I'm just supposed to fall in line with them and do what they say.

I have half a mind to tell him to go fuck himself and go up to my room like I planned, but I'm still feeling stir-crazy from being cooped up for so long, and... I'm a little curious what he's talking about. I have no idea what Black Roses do for fun, other than destroy people's lives, but it might be interesting to find out. Maybe.

"Fine," I say, letting out a breath. "Whatever."

Rory laughs. "Don't let us twist your arm, Hurricane. If you'd rather go up to your room and sulk, you can do that instead."

"Fuck off," I reply, but it's lacking a bit of heat.

126

Levi cracks a smile finally, and he seems interested in the idea of taking me out. Sloan, surprising no one, seems reluctant and displeased.

"Are you sure?" he asks Rory, pinning him with a look.

Rory just shrugs. "Sure, why not? She'll be fine, and we all do deserve a night out."

Sloan sighs and then nods once. "Fine."

With his agreement, we all get back in the car to head out again.

This time, we head to a part of town that I'm familiar with but haven't been around much before. It's less nice than the part with the university campus, and there aren't droves of college students hanging out drinking and smoking. It reminds me more of the area surrounding the warehouse where my dad trains and fights, and there are groups of people gathered on corners and near buildings, talking and laughing but clearly on their guard.

It's not the kind of place you'd want to end up in alone, definitely.

I live in a bad neighborhood, and Scarlett grew up in one that's pretty much the same. I've got enough street smarts to know that this isn't somewhere I'd want to be at night if I didn't have these three men with me.

Speaking of the assholes, all three of them seem as comfortable in this atmosphere as they do at their house, so I figure it can't be that bad if they brought me here. The Black Rose gang can clearly blend in anywhere in the city, from the fancy places where they need to have their expensive car valet parked, to run-down buildings that look like they're exclusively used for sketchy drug deals.

Must be nice to have that kind of confidence.

That kind of *power*.

We pull up to a building that looks like some abandoned warehouse but smaller from the outside, with no identifying markers other than the cars parked outside and the lights in the windows. I wonder if the Black Roses do anything important in places that *aren't* run down and creepy, but I keep that thought to myself. My thoughts drift back to the gas station they brought me to at the beginning of all of this, and I guess it makes sense for them to spend time and do their business in places where they don't have to worry about being bothered.

We go inside, and I glance around the space as we enter. There are a bunch of guys hanging out, sitting in chairs talking and playing cards. From the inside, it's clear that this is some kind of run-down training gym, and it's apparently where the Black Rose guys come to hang out and chill on the weekend or whenever.

There's nothing fancy or overstated about it either. Everything is old but serviceable, with a low counter off to the side where drinks are being made. It's mostly beer and dark liquor from what I can tell, and I grab a cup of something and follow the three of them farther in.

As soon as we walk in, people stop and greet the guys.

It makes sense, considering Sloan is the leader's son and all, and the other two seem just as well-known, either from their own reputations or because they come as some kind of package deal with Sloan.

A burly guy with a buzz cut and tattoos spreading from his neck down over his shoulders comes over and gives Rory a fist bump. He eyes me curiously and then flicks his gaze over to Sloan. I wonder when the last time was that some random girl got brought to this place, and I don't blame him for seeming slightly confused about my presence.

"This is Mercy," Rory tells him when Sloan doesn't seem inclined to say anything. "She's a friend of ours."

I snort but don't contradict him. It's probably better to keep my mouth shut about what's really going on if the rest of these guys don't already know.

"Hey," the man says, nodding. "Jesse."

I nod back, and a few others make their way over to satisfy their curiosity. Rory handles the introductions as the most open and sociable one of my three keepers, introducing me as their "friend" Mercy to everyone who comes forward. I pay close attention to every name, trying to associate them with faces and identifying marks, just in case I ever need that information.

There's a guy with dreads wound up into a bun at the top of his head. Another one with a blooming rose tattoo on his hand. Another with a scar through his eyebrow. I would have expected them to be more on their guard about a stranger in their midst, but it seems like they're all in chill mode, drinking and laughing and relaxed. And I guess since I came with the son of Gavin Kennedy and his two friends, I get a pass.

It makes me relax a little, even though I definitely plan to stay on my guard and keep my eyes open. I'd planned to spend tonight not thinking about the Black Rose gang or anything going on with them, but in the middle of their den, I have to change my plan.

After a few minutes, the three men lead me to a little circle where a couch and some chairs have been set up, and I sit down on the couch, sipping what tastes like rum and coke from my cup while glancing around at everything.

There's a pool table in one corner where a group is gathered around, laughing and joking while one of them steps up with the cue. The card game is still going on, a new hand being dealt while the dealer gives the players shit about losing all their money.

In the center of the room is a large ring, clearly for fighting, and I perk up even more when I see it. There's nothing like a good fight to really blow off some steam, and I'd even settle for just watching, since I'm not exactly dressed to get in the ring in my short dress from clubbing.

Rory and Levi plop down on either side of me, leaving Sloan to take one of the arm chairs, holding a drink in his hand. I'm sort of sandwiched in between the two of them, and I can feel the heat from their bodies and smell their cologne. Each time one of them shifts, they brush against me, and it's like those places are hyper sensitive, radiating the light touch through the rest of my body.

But that is *so* not what I want to be focusing on right now, so I shove it down, taking a large gulp from my cup to try to think about anything else.

It's a major win for me to be here, a chance I'd better take and make the most of. Maybe something good can still come out of tonight. After the embarrassing scene at Sapphire, the guys have brought me deeper into their world.

If I'm going to bring them all down, and I sure as fuck plan to, then I need to take advantage of it.

14

I'M NOT sure if it's carelessness or just confidence born from being in their own space that makes the Black Roses gathered around us talk freely about their business, but no one seems to care that I'm sitting there, nursing my drink and listening intently to every word they say.

Jesse, the big guy from earlier, makes his way over and sits down in one of the other chairs, giving Sloan a look as he lays out an encounter he had with two Jackals a few days ago.

"Truce seems to be coming apart at the seams," he says, shaking his head and swigging from his can of beer. "The fuckers aren't respecting the boundaries, and if they're gonna be in our space, they're gonna have to pay for it."

My ears perk up, but I keep my expression neutral, listening closely while trying to appear entirely disinterested. If they knew how curious I am about what they're saying, I have a feeling they'd be less inclined to talk around me. But if they don't think I give a shit, it's probably pretty easy to dismiss me.

The conversation continues, and with other people chiming in as well.

Jesse's assertion that the Jackals will have to pay if they keep encroaching on Black Rose territory seems to be the general consensus shared by the people around us. Apparently, the truce was already shaky at best, and there have been infractions coming from the Jackals' side for a while now.

Some of them seem eager and excited for the coming shit show that will no doubt pop off if the Jackals keep pushing things.

"It's been so long since I've had a good fight," one of them says, cracking his knuckles with a savage grin. "They got off too easy the last time. It's time to make them pay."

"Won't be a need for a truce if they're all dead," someone else echoes, and the two of them bump fists.

They're definitely not alone when it comes to wanting to go after their rivals after so much time pretending at peace, but there are also some members of the gang who seem more wary about getting into another turf war.

I can hear some of them murmuring about how dangerous it will be if the truce dissolves completely, and how they don't want to have to go back to being on their guard all the time.

A small shiver runs down my spine, and I work hard not to give away my thoughts. I remember a time when the two gangs were at war. It's been relatively peaceful for years, but when shit was bad between the Jackals and the Black Roses, *everyone* in Fairview Heights felt it.

Is another war really on the horizon?

Fuck, that could be really bad.

Rory and Levi don't really offer their opinions on the matter, but I assume they'd be ready to fight if they had to. Sloan just listens, leaning back in his chair with the usual intense look in his eyes. It's impossible to know what he's thinking, and I don't let my gaze linger on him for too long, not wanting to invite his attention back to me.

If I stay quiet and just listen, maybe they'll keep talking without noticing I'm there. Every scrap of information could help me reach my goal of getting some kind of leverage over these guys, and there's a part of me that hopes maybe one of them will say something that will tell me what's going on with my dad.

I don't really expect them to know, especially since most of these guys didn't seem to have a clue who I was when we walked in, but it's hard not to hope all the same.

At some point in the conversation, Levi gets up and comes back with more drinks. He passes a beer to Rory and hands me another cup. I glance at him and take it, drinking quickly to avoid thinking about him thinking about me.

I usually don't drink this much, and the shot from the club was a while ago at this point, but so was my last meal. I can feel the first drink burning under my skin still, and the second one just adds to it, filling my head with a pleasant buzz.

The voices of the men around me start to blur together as they talk about their business, and I keep my ears open to make sure I don't miss anything, but I'm definitely not as focused as I could be.

Luckily, the business talk doesn't last for much longer.

They're all drinking as well, talking shit to each other as the card and pool games resume, and then a few different guys step into the ring in the center, challenging each other to fights.

None of them are serious since they're all various levels of drunk at this point, and most of them just fuck around, tripping each other or going for the pin.

It's still entertaining as hell, especially considering I haven't seen anything even this close to a real fight since the one that got my dad in trouble.

The guys around us cheer and call out taunts and encouragement to the ones in the ring, and it's hard not to get swept up in the excitement in the room.

Everyone's loud and rowdy, stomping their feet and yelling mostly good-natured insults at each other. I'm paying attention to the ring, but it's hard to not be aware of Levi and Rory on either side of me at the same time.

They both smell really fucking good, like the cologne they put on and like themselves underneath it. I can't shake the scents, even with so many other people around and the smell of beer and cigarette smoke in the air too.

I have no idea if it's intentional or not, but I realize with a start that they're both touching me. Rory's the most blatant with a hand on my leg, barely above the knee as he leans forward to heckle the man in the ring who just got taken down by a man half his size. I can feel the heat from his fingers against my skin where the bottom of my dress has ridden up, and I have to swallow hard at the sensation.

Levi is more casual. He has his arm thrown across the back of the couch comfortably, but his hand is right at the side of my neck, fingers dangling so close that they're brushing against the skin there. Again, I can't be sure if he's doing it on purpose, but he almost seems like he's absently stroking the skin there while his eyes are trained on the ring.

I feel like I can hear my heartbeat over the chaos in the room, and it pounds through me as my arousal rises. I can't help it. My clit is throbbing gently, a needy ache building low in my belly, and I'm grateful I opted to wear a bra under my dress so my hard nipples aren't poking out for everyone to see. This close, with their hands on me, I'm flooded with memories of hooking up with Levi and rolling around on the gym floor with Rory.

All the remembered images and sensations blend together, making my face hot, and I'm so tempted to get up and get some air—but I know one or both of them would just follow me, which would defeat the purpose. So instead, I clench my thighs together tighter, which has the unfortunate side effect of shifting Rory's hand a bit higher, his pinky slipping under the hem of my dress just the slightest bit.

I stare at it for a second and then whip my gaze back up to the ring, trying to focus on something else. Drinking around these men was probably not the brightest idea I've ever had, but I finish my drink anyway and then lean forward to put the empty cup down on the low table in front of me.

When I lean back, it's like settling into the curve of Levi's arm, and this time his fingers are definitely stroking my skin lightly.

I stare hard at the fighters, sizing them up to force myself to think about something, *anything* other than the two of them and how close they are. I'm not even going to dare to look at Sloan at this point.

The two guys currently in the ring are about the same size, both big and built, around the same size as Rory. One of them is bald, and the other has close-cropped blond hair, so I nickname them Baldy and Blondie in my head and settle in to watch.

They square off, shit-talking each other about being too drunk to throw a punch, and then Blondie lashes out first, catching the other with a playful slap to the face.

I laugh along with everyone else, clapping my hands in encouragement. "Don't take that shit!" I shout. "Hit him back!"

"You heard the lady!" someone else agrees.

Baldy lunges forward to aim a punch, but Blondie ducks under his arm and elbows him in the stomach as he comes up on the other side of him.

It knocks Baldy for a loop for a second as he wheezes for breath, and I laugh out loud. "Oh, come on! This is pathetic!"

The people around us seem to be enjoying my commentary, laughing along and calling out that I'm right and they've seen better fights in pre-schools, but Baldy doesn't look like he's having a good time listening to me heckle him. His eyes narrow, not at me but at his opponent, and he goes in for another hit only to have it be blocked pretty easily.

The noise of frustration he makes is almost lost in the booing from the others gathered around, and I boo louder than the rest, getting swept up in the atmosphere of it all.

"I could do better than that, and I'm half his size," I say, talking to anyone around who's listening, which is basically everyone.

Rory is laughing his ass off, and even Levi has a little smile on his face, and it feels kind of nice to be a part of this whole thing. Almost normal, since it's the way I was raised by my dad. He always had me watching fights with him on TV, and when I got old enough that I could hold my own, he would bring me down to the ring to let me watch him train and then let me get in to train with him. It's always been a part of my life, and just watching has my blood humming with adrenaline, which makes it hard to shut up.

Besides, none of the others are holding back, so I don't see why I should either. When Blondie snaps his fist out and lands another hit, I whistle in appreciation and call out to him. "Go for the kill. This idiot is wide open!

Baldy whips his head around to glare at me. "Can you shut the fuck up?" he snaps, and I can see he's red-faced, either from anger or alcohol or probably both.

"Hey—" Someone interjects, but he silences them with a hard look.

"You're talkin' a lot of shit for someone sitting on the sidelines," Baldy says, and he seems pretty confident that he can say whatever he wants to me.

I'm not even angry, but I can feel the fire of the challenge burning hotter, the adrenaline taking over everything else. I smile sweetly at him, but it doesn't even come close to reaching my eyes.

"I'd be glad to climb in the ring and show you how it's done," I tell him. "You want to go?"

He looks pissed as shit, but his gaze slides to Sloan, obviously looking for permission or confirmation.

Fuck that. I'm on my feet in a second, blood buzzing from the alcohol and everything else I'm feeling.

"Don't look at him," I say. "If you have a problem with me, then you settle it with *me*. Sloan's not the fucking boss of me. I get to decide what I do, and I want to fight you."

Baldy still looks like he wants to say no, and I narrow my eyes, staring him down.

"What?" I taunt, voice sweeter than it's been all night. "Are you scared to fight a *girl*?"

The group around us inhales collectively, and Baldy glares right back at me. I can see that typical macho pride flare in his eyes, and I know I've got him. It always works, especially with these types. Every single fucking time.

"Fuck it," he growls angrily. "Let's go."

I grin and toe off my heels, leaving them by the couch. I'm still dressed up from our brief time at the club, and my tight dress is definitely not the kind of thing I'd choose to fight in, but it will have to do. Judging from what I saw when Baldy was fighting Blondie, this won't take long anyway.

I walk forward and hop into the ring, feeling the rough material under my bare feet. There's a thrill that comes with fighting, and it's similar enough to fucking that I'm hoping I can work off some of the energy that buzzes under my skin and stop thinking about Rory and Levi. Being out from between them definitely helps, and I take a deep breath and square off with my opponent, dropping into a fighting stance naturally.

Rory, Levi, and Sloan have seen me fight before, and Rory knows firsthand that I can hold my own. But the rest of these Black Roses? They don't know what to expect from me, and I can feel their energy and anticipation growing as they watch.

It's like I'm feeding on it, letting it hype me up, and it blends in with the adrenaline of staring down a man several inches taller than me and probably a hundred pounds heavier.

He's big. And he's pissed.

But I'm not worried. I'm a good fucking fighter. My dad taught me well, and I've proven that time and time again. It won't be any big thing to prove it again here tonight.

Baldy's standing there, clearly waiting for me to make the first move. So I do, dancing in close enough to throw a right hook his way, which he barely dodges back from. I grin and swipe out again with my left hand, catching him on the chin and earning myself surprised laughter from the crowd. I wait just a second to see if he's going to retaliate, and when he doesn't, I throw a couple more punches, catching him with each one.

The rage builds behind his eyes, and I stay on my toes, ready when he finally snaps his fist out, throwing a punch back at me. Remembering Rory's tip from before, I duck under it easily and move out of his reach.

Rory's moved up closer to get a good view of the fight, and I glance down at him, seeing something like pride flash in his eyes. Apparently he likes that.

Excitement surges through me, adding to the adrenaline already burning hot in my veins. For some reason, that look of pleased pride in Rory's green eyes does something to me. It makes me want to show off more, to prove to him what I can do.

So I keep fighting. Baldy's putting up more of a fight than I would've expected based on the performance he gave with Blondie. He learns as we go on, ducking and dodging back from my hits and trying to take me out with sweeps of his legs. He's not going to be an easy tap out the way I was expecting, so I adjust to match him, fighting more aggressively.

When he lands a hit to my stomach, I aim my knee for his balls, barely missing as he twists to avoid it. His movement makes it easy for me to get him in the back with my elbow, and he grunts in pain, making me smile viciously.

The gathered members of the gang are eating it all up, yelling and stomping, calling out to us. Some of them are on Baldy's side, telling him he can't let a little girl kick his ass, but a surprising number are for me, cheering and telling me to keep going.

I can hear a deafening whistle split through the noise, and Rory's voice calls out, "Kick his ass, Hurricane!"

I grin because I plan to do just that.

My blood is pounding under my skin, hot with the thrill of a good fight; it really is up there with sex for things that I love to do. Nothing takes me out of my head better than a rough and dirty tumble in the ring.

It's clear that most of the Black Roses aren't made for fighting like this. They know enough to grapple someone if they need to, and I bet they could all shoot a gun better than I can, but they haven't been trained for this. Not like me. Most of them who have been in the ring tonight have been keeping it to boxing, with some non-regulation moves, but I have different styles under my belt, and I plan to use them.

Baldy's built like a brick house, but I aim a kick for his knee, making him crumple a bit. I use that opening to launch myself at him, using a few MMA moves to get him down on the mat.

I grapple him, trying to stay on top. My dress is short enough that it just rides up as we fight on the mat, giving me enough range of motion to keep my edge.

Baldy bucks under me, trying to get up or turn the tables, but I don't let him, using all my weight to keep him pinned. I want to get this fucker into an arm bar and make him tap out.

As we tussle, hands and knees and limbs go everywhere. At some point in his struggle, Baldy manages to flip us, pinning me down, and his hand ends up on my ass. I can feel the heat of it through my underwear, and I move to try to get him off of me.

Before I can make much progress there, he's suddenly hauled up and off of me, and I have to blink up and blow hair out of my face to see what's going on.

Sloan is standing above me, eyes murderous with rage. He punches Baldy squarely in the face and drops him in one hit. The guy goes down like a sack of bricks, and Sloan makes it look effortless.

Fucking show-off.

I scramble to my feet. I can hear my pulse pounding in my ears, the blood still rushing through me, demanding I keep the fight going. I go to brush myself off, and I realize my skirt has completely ridden up, showing my ass to the entire gathered audience.

Shit. No wonder it was so easy for Baldy to get a hand on me. Good thing I put on nice panties before going out earlier, I guess.

Once I'm up, Sloan turns those furious eyes onto me, looking like he wants to rip me apart right here in front of everyone.

He's not the only one who's angry though, and I'm not about to be cowed by him.

Everything I try to do ends up like this—with him standing there looking at me like I've done something wrong, his jaw clenched tight and his shoulders tense.

But I'm not the asshole here. He is.

And I'm fed up with his shit.

Instead of giving him the satisfaction of saying anything or chewing me out in front of the entire crowd of men, I just flip him off and climb out of the ring, stalking away.

15

FUCK THIS SHIT.

I want nothing more than to leave and go home. I don't mean the guys' house, either. I want to go back to my *own* home and sleep in my own bed and scream into my own pillow about what a fucking asshole Sloan can be when he wants to.

And it seems like he always wants to.

Hell, I'd even settle for going back to their house and barricading myself in my room at this point. A shower to wash this night off sounds good, and I can call Scarlett and bitch about what a fucking dick I'm stuck with.

But I can't exactly leave since they're my fucking ride and I don't have a car of my own. I can't be in the main room with all of them for another second though, so I keep walking until I find the locker room at the back of the warehouse, down a long, dimly lit hall.

That will have to do. I walk in, slamming the door shut behind me while I try to calm down.

The door slams open again a second later, before I even have time to take a breath, and Sloan barges right in, still radiating his bad mood and looking pissed as shit.

"What the fuck was that?" he snaps, glaring at me like I'm some kind of misbehaving child.

"I could ask you the same damn thing," I shoot back. "I was fucking *winning*, and you had to get all up in my business. Jesus, I don't know why you can't just stay out of things. I can take care of myself."

Sloan laughs, but it's a harsh, cruel sound that has no real humor to it at all. "Right. I'm not so fucking sure that's true. You started the night off grinding on some handsy lech in a club and ended it by rolling around on the floor with your ass hanging out for every man in the place to see."

"So *what?*" I demand. "Why the fuck does it matter to you?"

I step forward, not backing down for a second, not even in the face of his anger. He's the kind of guy who seems like he's used to getting what he wants and having people be afraid of him, but that's not happening here. I don't care if he's angry. I'm just as pissed off. More, even. The adrenaline from the fight is still there, pushing me to finally have it out with Sloan for being a controlling, overbearing dick when no one asked him to.

There's something wild and feral in his icy gray eyes, and it's not just anger, I don't think. The tension that always seems to surge between us when we end up arguing rises up like a force of nature, and I don't back down from that either, leaning right into his space and letting the feeling carry me along.

"What the fuck is your problem, Sloan?" I press. "You don't like other men looking at me? Well, that's too fucking bad. You don't own me, and I can do whatever the hell I want."

I give him one last look and then march past him toward the door, ready to go back out there and prove it. Baldy's probably up by now, and if he isn't, I'll wake him up and make him give me another go.

I don't get that far though. A hand wraps around my wrist, tight as a vise, and Sloan yanks me back around to face him.

Our chests press together as I slam into him, our bodies colliding. My chest is heaving as I breathe through my anger, and Sloan's in the same boat. I can practically feel his pulse racing, and I know he can feel mine too.

The air is thick with the tension, snapping like lightning right before a storm. We stare at each other for a long moment, frozen in place, our eye contact charged with the same energy.

And then suddenly, he lunges forward and smashes his lips against mine.

That's the spark that lights the flame.

That's all it takes to burn us down.

I gasp softly in surprise but kiss him back. My hands go to his chest, fisting the fine material of his shirt and not giving a shit about leaving wrinkles behind.

We kiss wildly, viciously, as if we're each fighting against whatever this thing is and losing. His mouth tastes like whatever he was drinking, something smoky and dark and all too tempting, and even though I'm mad as hell at him, I can't help the way my body seems to fucking crave him. I want his hands on me. I want him to kiss me until I can't see straight, and I can't deny it anymore with him right there, giving me everything I've been holding back on.

The roar of my blood in my ears is even louder now, and I give in to it, pulling Sloan closer to me and giving as good as he does.

Even *this* is a battle of wills, because of course it is. We each fight for the upper hand, wanting to come out on top. I can taste the anger on his tongue when he shoves it into my mouth roughly, can feel the frustration coiled just under his skin, and it echoes the same feelings in me.

Arousal, irritation, and lust in equal measure.

I want to punch him right in his stupid face for being a surly, controlling asshole, but at the same time, I want to keep kissing him. It stokes that fire in me, and I groan into his mouth as we crash around the small locker room, stumbling into walls and barely avoiding tripping over the benches.

Sloan kicks over a trash can as we pass but doesn't stop to look. He has his hands on my lower back, and then they slide lower down to my ass, gripping hard through the thin material of my dress and panties, fingers digging in like he's staking his claim. At the same time, he bites down on my lower lip, tugging on it a bit, drawing pleasure like a sharp line through me as I gasp and arch closer against him.

I moan deeply before backing him up against the side of a locker and leaning up onto my toes to kiss him even harder, chasing his tongue with my own and teasing it until I can feel the tension in him ratchet up even higher.

He growls under his breath. We're both breathing hard, but neither of us seems to care very much about that, and neither of us is backing down either. It's not in our natures.

And for better or for worse, that translates to being really fucking hot in this scenario.

Sloan flips our positions, slamming me hard into the wall as his kisses trail from my mouth down to my neck. I can't help the gasp that spills from my lips, both from being pushed so hard and the way his mouth lights up the skin of my neck like electricity right there on the surface.

I'm wet. I can feel arousal soaking the crotch of my panties. Just his hands on me, his mouth on mine and on my neck have me already panting and hungry for more, and there's no hiding that.

When I look down Sloan's body, he can't hide his arousal either. His cock is already tenting his pants, and I want to grind against him and feel how big he is.

Sloan, in typical fashion, doesn't give me the chance. He kisses his way back up to my mouth, capturing it in another searing kiss that I can feel all the way to my fucking toes. He grabs my upper arms and hauls me over to the corner of the room where there's a sink built into a counter with a small, dingy mirror above it.

Before I can say anything, he pushes me over the counter so my ass is out and on display for him. With no shoes on, I have to go onto my toes slightly to keep the cheap plastic material of the counter from digging into my belly, and I know that puts my ass up even more in his line of sight.

"Fuck." Sloan swears under his breath, his voice harsh and ragged. When I glance up into the mirror, I can see him behind me, staring a hole through the back of my dress.

He wastes no time from there. His big hands find the hem of my dress, and he shoves it up over my ass, baring it all for him.

"Fuck," he says again, and this time he sounds angrier, but like he can't tell if he's mad at himself or mad at me. The muscles in his cheeks ripple as he clenches his jaw.

"You have no fucking idea what you did to me. Seeing you rolling around up there, ass out. You got me so fucking hard."

He's put out about it, clearly, but even the pissed off tone of his voice can't negate how hot it is to hear him say shit like that.

The low growl of his voice washes over me, almost like something tangible, and I can imagine him sitting in his chair glaring daggers at me while trying to hide how turned on he is. It's a hot image, if I'm being honest.

I swallow hard, but I'm never one to let a situation get out of my control. I'm not going to go to pieces just because of some dirty talk.

"Is that what your problem is? I thought you were so pissed off about my ass hanging out because it was unlady-like or some shit," I taunt him. "Turns out, you just couldn't handle seeing it and were about to come in your pants like a fucking teenager."

Despite my rude words, my voice is strained, and I know he can hear how close I am to unraveling. All my calm collectedness—as little as I had to begin with—has flown out the window, and all I want is for him to touch me or fuck me or *something*.

I won't beg for it, but it's on the tip of my tongue to tell him to get on with it, because being bent over and on display the way I am is doing nothing but turning me on more.

Sloan just snorts at my taunt, not seeming to give a single shit about what I have to say. He's staring with single-minded intensity at my ass, and I'm sure with the way my legs are spread to keep my balance, he has a great view of how wet my pussy is through my panties.

He groans. I've never heard anyone make a groan sound pissed off before, but Sloan has a talent for that shit, clearly. He drops down behind me, disappearing from the mirror, and I feel his fingers tugging my panties down so they wrap around my knees.

I hold my breath, and when those fingers probe at my wet pussy and spread the folds so he can have a better view, I suck in a lungful of air, immediately getting wetter.

There's one last muted curse from Sloan, and then he dives in, the flat of his tongue licking a searing hot line against my pussy.

He holds on to my thighs in a grip like iron, and I couldn't get away from him even if I wanted to. With him behind me and the sink in front of me, I'm trapped, and there's nothing to do but let him have what he wants.

What we both want, at this point.

His mouth is hot and wet, but not as wet as I am for him. He uses that grip to keep my legs open, and the panties around my knees won't let me spread them any wider. So I have to take what I can get, but I'm not complaining. Especially when Sloan slows his licking, teasing the edges of my entrance with the tip of his tongue in a way that sends shocks of pleasure through me.

I glance up, and I'm met with my own reflection.

My hair is a mess from the fight and the kissing, and I have to blow strands of it out of my face. My eyes are dark, an almost emerald green from the lust working its way through my body, and when Sloan trails his way down to flick his tongue against my clit, my lips part.

They're red and slightly swollen, and I know I look like I'm desperate for more. I half wish I could see Sloan's face, see how he looks when he's behind me, eating me out like I'm his last meal, but maybe it's for the best that I can't.

His fingers dig into my skin hard enough that I'm sure I'm going to have bruises tomorrow, and I can't bring myself to be mad about it. Not when he's lapping at me, working his tongue over my pussy in slow licks that alternate with a few quick ones.

"Sloan," I breathe, saying his name and almost wishing I could take it back.

It would be impossible for me to pretend that I'm not into this. He has a front-row seat for how fucking wet I am, and he can taste my arousal, I know. All the reasons I had in my mind about why this is a terrible idea are slipping away with every lick, every time his tongue passes over my center, and I wish he would slide inside it. All I can think about is how good it feels, and how I want more.

"Sloan," I moan again. "Fucking—stop teasing me."

He just snorts and doesn't do anything to speed up or slow down his pace. He stays on target, licking and sucking at my sopping wet folds, swirling his tongue around as he gets the lay of the land as it were and makes himself comfortable between my legs.

It's a steady pace, designed to keep me turned on and needy, apparently, and it's fucking working.

I push my ass back, trying to get him deeper, grinding on his face a bit, and he reaches up and slaps my ass in reprimand, the sound echoing around us in the otherwise empty locker room.

My moan echoes as well, and he dives back in, tongue dipping and swirling and laying claim while I shudder above him, fingers scraping against the smooth surface of the counter.

The sink is cool against my skin, a contrast to the heat of Sloan's mouth and the scrape of his stubble as he works himself deeper, licking into me finally.

I groan with relief, and each time his tongue slides in, I imagine it's something longer and thicker. Maybe after this it will be.

He fucks me with his tongue, spearing it in deeper and deeper, as deep as it will go, and I shake and nearly scream with pleasure, throwing a hand over my own mouth at the last second so it doesn't give us away. The rest of the gathered members of the gang are just down the hall, and if they hear me screaming, there will be no hiding what it is we're doing in here.

I don't know if Sloan wants that, but I sure as hell don't, so I try to keep my moans muffled. But it's harder than it should be with him going to town on my pussy like it's a feast.

I can hear the wet sounds of him lapping at my pussy, and it just adds to the debauched filthiness of this whole thing, the echoes of it bouncing around the room and mingling with the harsh rasp of my breathing.

Sloan's tongue retreats from inside me, and I frown and nearly look over my shoulder to tell him to get back to it.

Instead of withdrawing completely, though, he takes one hand from my thigh and slides it between my legs, letting his fingers glide through the wet mess I've made. I swallow hard, trembling a bit at how good that feels, and when those rough fingers find my clit, my knees nearly buckle.

It feels so good. It feels *better* than good, and my mouth falls open on a silent groan. He pushes his tongue back into me, licking me open with an aggression that's sexy as fuck.

His fingers move in time with his tongue, and it's almost too much. Almost. His mouth doesn't let up, and his fingers rub maddening circles against my clit in a way that whites out my brain for anything but the pleasure coursing through me.

It's impossible to ignore the way it takes over every-thing else, washing away the anger, the frustration, the need to keep quiet. It's so much, building and building until I can barely hold it in or hold it back.

Not that Sloan cares. He just keeps going, his mouth working overtime as he eats me out, his fingers moving with precision like he knows exactly where I'm the most sensitive and how to get me off. I'd be impressed if I had enough brain function left for anything other than attempting to process how good this feels.

His free hand comes up from my thigh to grab at my ass, spreading me open even more, making it so there's nowhere Sloan can't reach, and he takes full advantage of it, licking me like he wants to savor every drop.

"Fuck yes," I pant. "Just like that. Fucking—god, yes."

I can feel my orgasm building, starting with a searing heat in my core that spreads out, taking over my body. My legs shake and tremble just a bit, and if it weren't for the sink counter, I don't think I'd be able to stay standing. I don't know if Sloan can tell how close I am, or if he's just determined to wring every drop of pleasure he can get out of me, but he doesn't slow down even a little. He growls low, the sound lost in the wetness of my pussy, and he presses his fingers harder against my clit, rubbing it faster while he keeps working his stupidly talented tongue.

My mouth falls open, and I almost forget to breathe as sensations spike inside me. The pleasure is like a freight train barreling down on me, making it impossible to ignore as it sweeps me up and builds higher and higher and higher.

"Ahhh!"

A breathy whine pours from my lips, and I clamp my hand back over my mouth again, keeping the noises of my pleasure from getting too loud as best I can. It's so good, and I'm so close. I try to tell Sloan that, but I can't. I can't make any words come out of my mouth, and before I'm even able to brace myself for it, my orgasm hits me with full force. It knocks the wind from my lungs as I give in to it, head dropping low so I can't see myself in the mirror anymore.

My legs shake even harder as I fall apart, panting and still trying so desperately not to make too much noise as I come harder than I can remember coming in a while. I bite down on my palm to muffle the scream, but it still echoes a bit, just enough that Sloan will clearly know how easily he took me apart.

I'd be pissed about that, but it feels too good for me to fully care. The waves of pleasure keep washing over me, and I struggle to catch my breath as the sharp, hot sensation melts into something warm and sweet in my veins, washing away the lingering adrenaline and replacing it with something milder, more like satisfaction.

Sloan is still his same intense self, of course, and he doesn't give me a moment to relax. He surges to his feet and hauls me up by the back of my dress, then spins me around to face him. His eyes are dark, pupils blown wide, and I can see my own arousal shining on his lips and cheeks from where his face was buried against me.

He looks like he's nowhere near done, that hunger burning in his eyes growing like a thundercloud around him. He looks like he might fuck me right here and now, against the sink, with no regard for its structural integrity, and I want it.

Fuck, I want it.

I don't even care how insane it is.

Before I can say anything, he's pulling me in and kissing me deeply. I can taste myself on his lips, on his tongue when he slides it into my mouth and lets it tangle with mine. That tangy taste of my own arousal mingles with the flavor of his mouth, making liquid heat slide through my veins.

It's hotter than it really has any right to be, and I moan into it, pressing closer against him, seeking out more.

It's nothing like the furious making out we did before, throwing each other against lockers and walls. There's not quite as much hate and spite in this kiss either. It's not a battle of wills. Instead, it's deeper and more... something. I can't put my finger on it, but it stokes the fire inside me and has me grinding forward against him, wanting more even though I just came.

I don't want to think about the specifics or whatever

feelings are lurking under the surface. I just want to focus on the feeling of his body against mine, the way he's hard and firm, and not just because of his musculature. When he jerks his hips forward, I can feel the press of his cock in his nice pants, and my mouth waters.

I want to see it. I want to touch it and feel it inside me. All the denial from the last couple of weeks is coming crashing down around me, and I'm so close to demanding he give me what I need. It's my turn to growl into the kiss as it heats up, fingers sliding down his chest and stomach to the fly of his pants so I can undo them and pull his cock out.

We're lost in each other, his hands roaming up my back and down to grip my ass, hauling me in even closer. The sound of the door opening is very distant, but it still catches our attention.

I open my eyes to see Levi standing there, eyebrows nearly in his hairline as he watches us kiss and grind against each other.

My dress is still up around my hips, panties down around my ankles now, and my hand is practically in Sloan's pants. We both freeze for a second, one hundred percent busted.

Then Sloan shoves me away, knocking me back into the sink. He wipes his mouth and adjusts his pants like he's trying to hide the fact that he's hard as hell. It doesn't work, but he doesn't seem to care.

"We're going home," he snarls, the anger back in his voice. "We're fucking done here."

Levi and I both just stand there as he straightens his shirt and then marches out of the locker room without looking back at either of us.

16

I STAND THERE awkwardly once Sloan lets the door slam behind him. I know I look like a fucking mess, and there's no hiding what we were just doing.

Levi looks surprised and... almost jealous.

There's something in his eyes when he looks at me, a flash of envy that catches me off guard before he manages to school his expression into something more casual.

He shifts his posture, trying to look like he doesn't give a shit, but I know that's not fucking true. I saw that split second of feeling, and I have no idea what it means.

I don't know what the fuck is going on with me and these guys. I should hate them, I keep telling myself that I *do* hate them, but for some reason, they make me lose all common sense. The very things that piss me off the most somehow end up being the same things that catch my attention, and it feels like a never-ending cycle.

The last thing I should be doing is lusting after them or letting them get under my skin the way they do, but I just can't help it. I can still feel the phantom touches from Sloan along my skin, still feel the lingering thrums of pleasure from my orgasm, and there's a bit of disappointment there too—that Levi walked in before Sloan got the chance to fuck me.

That's a step too far though. That would be too fucking stupid and insane, and I shake myself, trying not to go down that path of thought. Instead, I fix my clothes, pulling my panties back up and my dress back down. I run the fingers of one hand through my dark hair, trying to make it look less messy and sex-tousled.

"What?" I demand of Levi, when it's clear he's not going to say anything first. "Do you have a problem? Something you want to say to me?"

He looks at me for a second longer, then shakes his head. "Nope. Just wondering where you two went off to."

"Well, here I am," I reply, striding past him.

"Yeah. I can see that."

We step out into the hall and walk back to the main room in silence. Most of the crowd has broken up at that point, and Baldy is nowhere to be seen. Guess he woke up and slunk off somewhere to soothe his bruised ego.

A few of the men who are still hanging out clap when they see me, and for a heart-stopping second, I think they know exactly what Sloan and I just did. Then Blondie grins and toasts me with his beer.

"Nice fight. You know how to hold your own," he says loudly, and the others agree.

Thank fuck.

I slip into my shoes and smile at them. Sloan is standing by the door, his usual thundercloud of anger and irritation swirling around him, and Rory meets us as we head toward him.

He claps me on the shoulder, eyes bright with good humor, and I don't shy away for a second. I can still feel Levi's gaze on me, burning a hole into my back, and I'm so tempted to whip around and ask him what his problem is, but I'm too tired to get into it with him.

The temporary peace doesn't last long though. We're about halfway to the car when Levi finds his voice.

"So, Sloan and Mercy were fucking in the locker room," he says mildly.

Rory's head snaps around to stare at him. "They were what?"

"Fucking. Probably. When I walked in they were making out like a couple of horny teenagers at the prom."

I glare at Levi for blabbing my business, and for being a fucking hypocrite. I don't know why he gives a shit if Sloan and I hooked up, especially considering he likes to act like it doesn't matter that he and I hooked up first. I don't even know if the other guys know about that, and here he is running his mouth about things that have nothing to do with him.

The anger that was washed away by a good orgasm comes back to the surface. For fuck's sake, it seems like I'm always going to be either pissed off or turned on around these assholes. Impulse takes hold, and I go with it, turning to face Rory and grabbing him by the shirt.

He has just enough time to give me a surprised look before I yank him closer and kiss him hard. For a second, he's stiff and unyielding against me, like he's not sure what to do with this new development. And then he's kissing me back, leaning down into it with a pleased sound low in his throat.

It's a good kiss, and it immediately reminds me of rolling around on the floor of their home gym, trying to get the upper hand and grinding against Rory's cock at the same time. I can feel my cheeks flushing, the heat from earlier flaring up, and I can only hope that it's dark enough out that none of them can tell. I already smell like sex anyway, so hopefully they won't notice that my already soaked panties just got even wetter.

"All right, that's enough. All of you, get in the fucking car." Sloan's voice cracks out like a whip to ruin the moment.

Rory's grinning like a loon when I pull away from him, and I pin Levi with a look, hoping he got the message.

I don't belong to anyone. Not to Sloan. Not to Levi.

Not to Rory. *I* decide who I kiss and when, and none of these guys have the right to try to dictate what I do.

Levi stares back at me, his brown eyes burning in the darkness. I think for a second that he might say something, and I brace myself for whatever it might be. But he just turns away, opening the door and sliding into the front passenger seat of the car, and I roll my eyes. Of all the guys, Rory is the most easygoing, and he doesn't seem to be all that upset about being used as a demonstration of my sexual independence.

His green eyes are a little heated when his gaze slides over me though, and I can see him adjusting his boner before he slides into the car, leaving me to climb in after him.

The drive back to the house is quiet, and I'm grateful as hell for that. I can feel a headache brewing, and the last thing I want to do is keep arguing with the three of these infuriating men.

Still, there's some smug satisfaction in knowing that at least two of them have blue balls. Maybe even all three if Levi's little tantrum is any indication. *Good.* They deserve it for being so irritating and not letting me have any privacy or agency or fun.

But then I lean back, getting comfortable in the seat, and I'm reminded of the ache in my own core, the need for more even though I already came earlier. I remember how hard Sloan was in his pants and how I really, really wanted him to fuck me in that moment, insatiable and eager for more, even though I didn't want to be.

Just thinking about it kicks the fire in my veins back into a full blaze. Unfulfilled desire rages through my body, and my heart beats a bit faster, not letting me forget about it.

So, okay, maybe there are *four* people in the car who are sexually frustrated right now.

Ugh. I have to do better.

I have to keep my walls up and make that shit airtight. I've been letting them get under my skin way too easily, and that's not acceptable. I can't keep slipping up around them just because they're hot and confident and too cocky for their own good.

That's even more of a reason to keep them out and make sure they don't get past my defenses or work their way under my skin. I'm trying to accomplish something, trying to make sure I can take them down, and I have to be strong. Nothing is more important than that, and I'll keep reminding myself as often as I have to.

I cross my arms and stare out the window, ignoring all of them. I can feel Rory looking at me every once in a while, but I don't look back. I will the arousal flaring inside me back down, putting the lid on it because it's not going to happen.

And I'm definitely not going to give in and touch myself in the shower tonight. That would be admitting defeat, and I never do that. I can be stronger than this, stronger than the low hum of need that seems determined to keep me on edge.

I have to be.

As soon as we get back to the house, I march past the guys and up the stairs, escaping to my room finally. I breathe a sigh of relief and slump against the closed door for a minute, glad to be away from them and on my own again. I think about showering to clear my head, but I'm too tired to make it all the way to the bathroom.

Instead, I change out of my dress and put on a fresh pair of panties and a tank top, happy to be comfortable. I text Scarlett that we're back at the house, then put my phone on the nightstand to charge before turning out the light.

The bed is soft under me, and the pillows are calling my name. Maybe I just need a good night's sleep, and I can try to forget this whole debacle of an evening ever happened. Or at least work on guarding myself against it ever happening again. I'll definitely settle for that if it's the best I can get.

I'm about to slide under the covers when the door to my room opens. My head snaps toward it as I sit up, my muscles tensing and my body instantly in fight-or-flight mode—which for me is basically "fight mode." I'm about two seconds away from ripping into whoever it is who thinks they can just barge into my room without knocking, but Levi comes striding in with a purpose.

The words die in my throat before they can come out, and I blink at him, surprised. He walks right up to the bed and grabs my face in his hands.

I have a split second to think about how warm they are before he's leaning in and kissing me. It's just a short kiss, nothing too hot or heavy, but it takes me by surprise. It's enough to open the floodgates on the memories of our hookup that I've been trying not to think about, and suddenly, I'm drowning in them.

In vividly captured images.

In memories I've never been able to forget.

His hands on me, touching me everywhere. Him pulling me closer, easing his cock into my body. His lips on my mouth, my neck, my breasts. The way he laughed when I demanded more, but then gave it to me anyway.

It's all I can think about for a second, and before I have a chance to either kiss him back or shove him away, he lets me go and steps back, half hidden in the shadows of the dark room.

We stare at each other for a second in the dim light, and I know my face is red, lips parted. I've been kissed more times tonight than I had in a while before this, and my head is spinning a bit.

Levi licks his lips. It's so dark in my room that his face

is painted in shadows, but I can see the gleam of his eyes disappear and then reappear as he blinks once.

"I wanted more," he says in a low voice. "I did. Just so you know."

Before I can say or do anything in response to that, he leaves just as quickly as he came in.

I'm left sitting on the bed, mouth open, staring at the closed door Levi disappeared through. He meant the time we were together before, I know that much.

He wanted more.

Of me.

Of us.

Fuck, what a mess.

The calm I've been struggling to hold on to is shattered now, and I just sigh and get into bed properly, pulling the covers up over my head and punching at my pillows like they'll somehow give up the answers to all my problems.

You have to do better, Mercy. You have to.

I say it over and over again to myself. I need to add more layers to the armor around my heart if I'm going to get through this. Because somehow, no matter how much I try to hate them, these guys keep breaking through.

17

ANOTHER WEEK GOES by pretty quickly, and I do my best to stick to my resolutions. I keep my distance from all the guys when I can and try to be emotionally distant when I can't.

Sloan makes that pretty easy, since he doesn't seem to want to look me in the eye after what happened between us in that locker room, and I'm happy to ignore him right back. Levi's still stalking me around my campus, but neither of us are very talkative. The car rides to and from school are quiet, and I can tell he's just as much in his head as I am. I'm grateful for that, because I don't want to talk about the kiss or the night at their gym hangout ever again.

Rory seems amused by the whole thing, but he doesn't push me, letting me ignore him when we happen to be in the kitchen at the same time and not teasing me as much as he would normally. I'm not sure why he's taking it so easy on me, but I'm not going to overthink it.

I have more important things to focus on. Like my dad. I'm getting more and more worried about him with every day that passes. It's been over three weeks now, and I haven't heard anything from him since that text he sent the day after I came to live with the guys. I can only hope whatever task Sloan's dad gave him isn't too dangerous, and he can manage to complete it.

But it's taking a long time, and I don't know if that's normal or if it means something's gone wrong. I don't want to call and bother him, especially if he's doing something that needs his focus, but I'm worried as fuck.

I lie in bed at night, thinking about how I wish there was something more I could do, something that would help speed things up. I want him to be safe, but also this is the longest we've ever gone without talking. We haven't spoken since the night of his fight, weeks ago now, and I miss him like hell.

He's been all I have for so long. I have Scarlett, of course, but Dad is my family. It's been the two of us since my mom died, and thinking about him out there, doing whatever he's been charged to do by the Black Roses, all alone, makes my heart hurt.

I need to do better here on my end. I need to find out more about the men I'm stuck with, in case there's anything that can help me help Dad. This thing isn't over yet, and neither of us will be safe until we're completely out from under the thumb of the Black Rose gang.

During the week, I have classes, and the guys do whatever it is they do. They come and go as they like, and there's not much time for me to really dig into anything.

But on the weekends, there's more wiggle room.

I've noticed over the time I've spent here that Rory tends to leave the house often by himself. There's even a set schedule to it, if I'm guessing right, and he goes somewhere alone for several hours three or four times a week.

Usually when I'm done with classes, he's just getting back, but on Saturdays it's easier to see when he leaves in the late morning and comes back sometime after dinner.

It's like clockwork, and I want to know where he's going. If it has anything to do with my dad, or even if it's just Black Rose business, I want to know what it is. The only upside of having to stay with these guys is getting the chance to learn their closely guarded secrets.

I can't just flat out ask him, because there's nothing subtle about that, so on Saturday, I wait for him to leave, thankful that Sloan seems to be off somewhere himself and Levi is in the gym.

Once I hear his car start outside, I count to five and wait for him to pull away. Then I slip out of the house and grab my bike, which the guys made good on having someone bring over, thank fuck.

I ride after Rory's car at a distance, trying not to be seen.

He's not driving in a way that seems sketchy or like he doesn't want to be followed at all, just like he has somewhere to be, and I narrow my eyes and keep going.

After about thirty minutes of driving, he parks on the street in a nice neighborhood and gets out of the car like he's about to walk the rest of the way to wherever he's going. I leave my bike a bit away from his car and follow on foot too, trying to be quiet so he won't be able to tell I'm there.

We're a long way away from the heart of Fairview Heights, and the neighborhood has a suburban feel to it. I walk past nice, well-built houses, the kind with real lawns and porches with swings. No one else is out, and it's a quiet late morning. Luckily, the streets are lined with trees, making it easy to hide behind them and peek out to make sure I can still see Rory.

Or at least, I *could* see him. About a block away from his car, he turns down an intersecting side street, but I wait too long to follow him. By the time I make it around the corner after him, he's nowhere in sight.

Fuck.

I press my lips together and scan the sidewalk, cursing inside my head.

Where the fuck did he go? He was right there, and then—

Before I can finish that thought, a hand clamps around my wrist as someone grabs me, yanking me around to face them. I yelp in surprise, adrenaline spiking. I've got my fist raised, ready to fight back, when I realize it's Rory. Shit.

He sees the look of recognition in my eyes as my fist lowers slightly, and he must know I'm not about to punch him. Still, he pins my arms and leans in, brushing his lips against the shell of my ear.

"You're a pretty fucking bad spy, you know that?" he murmurs, and he sounds almost amused by it.

Motherfucker.

Clearly, he knows exactly what I'm doing here, and I give up the fight, going limp in his arms with a little sigh. I figure he's going to send me back to the house, or tell Sloan I snuck out and let him deal with me, but instead, he lets me go and steps back, giving me a once-over.

"What the fuck are you doing, Mercy?" he asks, folding his arms. "You're supposed to be at the house."

He says it like he's talking to a wayward kid that snuck out after curfew or something, and I glare up at him, immediately getting defensive.

"I was just curious," I tell him. "You disappear all the time, and for all I know you're running drugs or something."

True to form, Rory just chuckles. "Come on," he says, shaking his head. "Come with me."

My eyebrows shoot up immediately.

I half expected him to make me turn around and head right back to the house, or lock me in the car if he wasn't going to take me there himself. Especially since I snuck out and followed him, getting all up in his business when I'm supposed to be at their house unless I have an escort or whatever.

But I'm not about to question it. I don't want him to send me back to the house, and this might be a chance to learn more about him. So I follow, glancing around at the neighborhood we're in and taking it in more than I did when I was following him.

It's different from the place I grew up in, and even different from the area where the guys' house is. This is more homey, a place where people probably raise families. Where their kids can play in the yards and swim in little backyard pools. It's like one of those neighborhoods from a sitcom or something, and I've never really spent much time anywhere like this before.

Rory walks toward a nice house, a little smaller than the ones around it, but well-maintained all the same. There's a little garden out front, and flowers in the window boxes. The front door is painted a sunny shade of yellow, and it looks warm and inviting.

I hesitate as we walk up the driveway, my eyes narrowing, and Rory turns around to grin at me.

"You wanted to see where I'm going." He gestures to

the yellow front door. "This is it. Come on, Hurricane, you're not chickening out now, are you?"

I glare at him because his smug grin makes me want to hit him in the face, but of course that's not a new feeling. He's always saying the exact right thing to get under my skin, and I let out a huffed breath and roll my eyes.

"Yeah, yeah. I'm coming," I shoot back, and he just smirks at me and then goes up to the door.

I wonder if he's going to knock or if he has a key. What the hell is this place? For all the reasons I try to come up with for Rory to be coming here, I can't wrap my head around who or what might be on the other side of that door.

When it opens before he has a chance to do anything more than step onto the front stoop, I'm surprised by what I see. Or *who* I see, I guess. Somehow, the last thing I expected was a gorgeous woman with rich red hair, standing there with a grin on her face.

"It's about time you got here," she says, hands on her hips for a second. "I was about to send out a search party. In case you got lost."

Rory rolls his eyes, but there's clear affection in his face as he looks at her. She looks about the same age as him, just a couple of years over twenty or so, and her smile is bright as she reaches out to hug him.

To my surprise, Rory lets her, and I can feel myself bristling. I don't want to, because it's no fucking business of mine who Rory wants to hug. It's his life, and he doesn't owe me anything. I don't have any connection to him other than basically being his captive, and I don't want to.

But that doesn't explain what we're doing here. If this is a hookup or something, then why the hell would Rory have brought me along? Is he showing off? Making it clear that even if I don't want him—and I don't—he has other women who do?

I can feel the annoyance building, and I want to demand that he tell me what the hell is going on, but I feel like I can't say anything, standing there listening to the two of them banter lightly before the woman turns to me.

"Who's your friend, Rory?" she asks, head tipped to one side.

"This is Mercy," Rory says. "She's hanging out with me today."

The woman gives me the same sort of sunny smile she gave him, and I feel a little bit bad for not liking her. It's not her fault Rory's an asshole and I'm confused.

"Hey. It's nice to meet you, Mercy," she says, reaching out to shake my hand. "I didn't even know Rory had other friends, so it's nice to see him with some company for once."

I blink in surprise, because Rory's never really alone, considering he lives with Sloan and Levi. And he's got a bunch of buddies in the Black Rose gang. But maybe she doesn't know about them? I have no idea what to say, so I just smile awkwardly back and follow the two of them into the house.

The front room is nice and airy, and the furniture looks comfortable and lived in. A few toys are scattered here and there, and I frown, really confused now.

There's a little shriek of happiness from down the hall, and suddenly, a blur of a little girl comes barreling into the room and throws herself into Rory's arms. She looks like she's maybe three or four, small and obviously delighted to see him.

And Rory just scoops her right up with a whoop, swinging her around and dropping kisses to the top of her head and her cheeks. They both laugh together as I watch, staring in shock.

Finally, Rory turns back to me, his eyes bright. "Mercy," he says. "This is Piper. My daughter."

18

MY DAUGHTER.

It takes a second for those words to process in my head, and I just gape at him in the meantime, probably looking like an idiot while I try to wrap my mind around it.

This is *so* not what I was expecting when I thought he was keeping a secret, leaving the house on his own all the time. An affair with a gorgeous woman? Some kind of criminal activity? Sure.

But... a daughter?

I'm stunned, and I know it shows on my face.

What I hope is *less* apparent is the way I feel like my ovaries might have just exploded. Because watching him hold a fucking kid like that, like she means the world to him, somehow makes his tattooed, built hotness even fucking hotter. I'm not even sure how that's possible, but there it is. I've never even been a baby crazy kind of girl.

Plenty of the girls I went to high school with were all about babies and men with children and thinking they were sexy as hell, but I never really got it.

Until right this moment.

Now I can kind of see where they were coming from, and that's as much of a surprise as the rest of this is.

The redheaded woman laughs softly and steps forward. "I'm Jen, by the way," she says, politely choosing to ignore the fact that my mouth is open wide enough for a bat to fly into it. "Figured I should introduce myself since Rory loses sight of everything, including his manners, when Piper's around."

"Nice to meet you." I shake her hand a little robotically, still trying to regain my footing.

She grins at me, her expression friendly and open. When we both turn back to look at Rory and Piper, she shakes her head a little. "You know, it's really not fair for you to be such a hot dad. You're going to give someone an aneurysm one of these days."

Something about the way she says that, and the way she talks to him in general, makes me feel like she's not interested in Rory herself. It's playful and teasing, but not flirtatious at all. More like how roommates or very close friends might talk to each other, but there's nothing more than that there.

I clamp my jaw shut, refusing to either confirm or deny Rory being a hot dad, but there's something about the way

Jen looks at me that makes me positive she already knows how I feel. And that's... fine, I guess. I mean, objectively, Rory is a delicious fucking specimen of manhood, so denying that would be a waste of time.

"And your name is Mercy, Rory said?" she asks, continuing on with the conversation. She's doing one hundred percent of the heavy lifting in this interaction since I'm still too shell-shocked to offer up any conversation of my own.

I nod, trying to snap myself out of the surprised stupor I'm in.

"How do you two know each other?" Jen looks between the two of us, and I glance over at Rory to see what he's going to say. I'm not exactly going to lay out how he and his friends basically kidnapped me in front of his daughter.

"We met through Black Rose stuff," he says and leaves it at that.

Jen just nods knowingly and doesn't ask anything else. So clearly she knows *something* about what he does and who his friends are, but it doesn't seem to be a topic they really discuss in much depth. Interesting.

She leans in and gives Piper a kiss on the cheek. "Do you think you can hold down the fort for a bit while I run out?" she asks, glancing up at Rory. "Amanda wanted to get lunch at that new sushi place downtown today."

"Yeah, of course." He shifts his daughter on his hip, grinning. "I've got it."

"You're a gem." Jen reaches out to pinch his cheek.

He gives her a look and bats her away with his free hand. "You're a menace."

"Oh, stop. You'd be lost without me." Jen turns to look at me, a grin stretching her features. "Don't take any of his crap, okay? He always likes to pretend he knows everything, but that's just an act."

I can't help but grin back at her. I like her already. "I won't," I promise. "I'm getting pretty good at seeing through him."

She nods approvingly and then dashes out, leaving the two of us—or rather, the *three* of us—alone.

Piper blinks at me once her mother leaves, and I blink back at her, not really sure how to interact with her. My experience with kids is pretty much nil, and I'm more nervous about having a conversation with her than I was about getting into the ring with Baldy that night at the Black Rose training gym.

Luckily, Rory steps in to fill the silence, giving the little girl a squeeze and then putting her down.

"Piper, this is my friend Mercy," he says. "She's going to hang out with us today. Are you okay with that?"

She nods, looking a little shy but peering up at me curiously. I can see Rory in her for sure—in the way her eyes gleam, and how she isn't afraid of some stranger in her home. She smiles a little and offers a wave before sticking her thumb in her mouth, and I can't help but smile back.

She's adorable, and it's so obvious that she loves Rory and he loves her right back.

"Lunch time, I think. No sushi like your mom, but we'll see what we can get for you, okay?"

Piper nods enthusiastically, and they head to the kitchen. I follow a few steps behind, still trying to get my brain to catch up with everything that's happening here.

Rory has a daughter.

One he spends a lot of time with, if he's coming here every time he leaves the house on his own. I was quick to assume it was something shady, some gang business or whatever, but instead it's something so completely... wholesome.

Fucking weird.

I watch him rummage through the refrigerator for a second and come out with some milk and a block of cheese. "How do we feel about mac and cheese?" he asks, addressing Piper, though his eyes flick to me.

"Yes!" the little girl says, bouncing excitedly on the chair she's climbed up onto.

Rory lifts an eyebrow at me, and I nod. Apparently I'm a part of the *we* now. "Sure. I haven't eaten lunch yet."

"Too busy sneaking around to eat, I guess," he says, but his grin is teasing. He doesn't seem all that upset about it, and I can't quite figure out why. I keep waiting for the other shoe to drop, for him to get on my case for following him here.

But he doesn't. Maybe he just doesn't want to fight in front of his daughter.

He moves around the kitchen with the same confidence and ease he has in the kitchen back at the guys' house, and I watch as he fills a pot with water and puts it on the stove before hunting down a cheese grater to start shredding the block of cheddar.

Watching him cook does nothing to make me less turned on than I already am, and desire simmers under the surface of my skin, no matter how hard I try to ignore it.

This is a different side of him, and yet it *isn't* at the same time. He's always been sort of domestic, usually in the kitchen, making food or coffee, leaning against the counter and cracking jokes. I see him in there more than I see the other two, and I realize that I've sort of been thinking of it as his domain.

While he works, he makes faces at Piper and asks her questions about her day.

"Mr. Twinkle got..." Piper frowns like she's searching for a word. "Permoted?"

"*Pro*moted," Rory corrects with a smile. "That's good for Mr. Twinkle. Isn't it, Mercy?"

I nod, impressed that the little girl knows a word like that, even if she said it wrong. "Very impressive. What did he get promoted to? And from?"

She's still shy when she looks at me, but it's clear she's happy we're engaging with her about who or whatever

Mr. Twinkle is. "Boss to Big Boss," she says. "He works hard."

Rory nods solemnly. "Then it's important that he got bumped up. I hope you offered him a generous raise to go with his new title."

"Six cookies," she says, beaming and holding up her fingers to show us.

"*Six*? Dang. Maybe I should think about switching careers if working for you pays that well. I'm on a three cookie salary."

I can't help but laugh as he teases her, grinning while his hands never stop moving. It's so clear that he loves his daughter. He's always silly and playful, but there's a different edge to it here, more loving than how he acts around the rest of us. Which makes sense.

It's a *disaster* for me, because while I sit here and watch, chiming in when asked something, I realize that the confusing pull I feel toward him isn't just sexual attraction anymore. That was hard enough to deal with, but now I'm actually starting to fucking like this guy.

Shit.

He turns to add the cheese to the simmering pot on the stove, and I can't help myself. My curiosity is killing me.

"So, what's the story here?" I ask.

I half expect Rory to make a joke or say something flippant to deflect, but when he turns back, he's giving me a

186

considering look. "Hold that thought," he says. "And watch this pot while you're at it."

"I can't cook for shi—" I cut myself off, glancing over at Piper. "Anything. I can't cook for anything."

"You don't have to cook." He shakes his head, grinning. "Just make sure it doesn't boil over. If the bubbles start going, turn it down. Stir it a little. I have absolute faith in you, Hurricane." He winks and steps away from the stove, ruffling Piper's hair as he moves past where she's sitting and then disappears into the living room.

I grumble under my breath but walk over to the stove and peer into the pot of cheese sauce. It smells good, and I give it a slight stir. Piper seems content to hum to herself at the table, her little legs swinging as we both wait for her father to get back.

It's only a minute or so later when Rory comes back, arms full of coloring books with a huge box of crayons balanced on top. He presents them to Piper who claps enthusiastically and reaches to take the box from him, setting it on the table. Rory puts the coloring books down on the table too and then sweeps a silly bow, eyes bright.

"Your entertainment, Your Highness," he says, dropping a kiss to the top of her head before he comes back over to where he left me with the pot. As he walks behind me, sliding into the space between me and the island, his hand brushes the small of my back, just lightly enough that I can't tell if it was an accident or not.

I jump slightly and go back to stirring, cheeks turning red.

"It's fine," I say, a little defensive on instinct. "It's not burned."

His smile softens a bit, and he shoos me away from the pot, taking the spoon and stirring the sauce himself. "I trusted you could manage not to burn the house down for a minute, Hurricane, don't worry."

I roll my eyes at him but don't go back to my seat at the island. Instead, I lean against the counter, my gaze flicking from Piper, who is happily coloring in one of the books, back to Rory.

He catches the look and shrugs a shoulder. "Jen and I dated for a while, but it wasn't anything really serious," he says, answering a question I had before but wasn't going to ask out loud. "She's great, really great, but it just wasn't going to work out. But when she got pregnant, I promised I was going to be there for her no matter what she decided to do. I went with her to all her appointments, sat in the car if she wanted to go in alone. Bought her so many weird fucking foods when she was having those pregnancy cravings."

"And you never thought about getting married or anything?" I ask. I don't mean it in a judgmental way at all, I'm just curious.

Rory seems to recognize that, and he shakes his head. "Nah. I mean, we thought about it for a hot second, but it wasn't going to be worth it. We don't love each other, you know? And a kid deserves to see their parents really in love, even if that's with other people and not each other."

"Oh," I reply, surprised at the sudden bout of seriousness from him.

I've only seen him without the teasing glint in his eyes a few times since I've met him. He speaks with gravity and conviction, like it's something he and Jen had a lot of long talks about, and it makes me see him in yet another light. It's been a big day for surprises, and seeing this side of Rory is... interesting, to say the least.

He shrugs again, gazing down at the cheese sauce as he stirs. "I look out for them. Jen and Piper. And I'm in Piper's life and make sure they have everything they need."

"And the Black Rose stuff?" I ask because I can't help myself. "Jen seemed to know a little bit about it, at least."

"Yeah. She knows I'm in the gang," Rory answers. "No way around that, really. But I try to keep distance between that business and Jen. Just to keep her insulated from that life and everything that goes along with it. She has her own stuff going on, and I don't want her to get mixed up with this kind of shit."

That's fair, and honestly kind of noble. I furrow my brow and find myself watching Rory as he finishes cooking, dumping the cooked pasta in the cheese sauce and adding some extra seasonings. He tastes a bite off the spoon and inhales through his mouth when it burns his tongue, and I snort a laugh, shaking my head at him.

"Try some," he coaxes, holding the spoon out to me. I shake my head again, backing away from the dripping cheese.

"Maybe when it's not molten magma hot."

Rory rolls his eyes. "I thought you lived on the edge, Hurricane. I thought you weren't afraid of anything."

"Not wanting to burn my tastebuds off has nothing to do with being afraid, Rory," I reply, deadpan.

He just laughs and grates some cheese over the top of the pot before dishing up three bowls of creamy, cheesy goodness.

Piper immediately clears space in front of her for the bowl when Rory brings it over, and she claps her hands happily for mac and cheese. I understand the sentiment. Once it's cooled down some, I take a bite, and of course, it's delicious.

Rory smiles as he watches me eat it, but then goes back to his own bowl, shoveling a few bites in before he starts asking Piper about what she colored.

Piper seems happy to talk about her art and then launch into a conversation about the promotion of Mr. Twinkle, who I learn is a giant stuffed cat that sits on the foot of her bed and makes sure nothing can crawl out from under it.

It's cute, the way she talks so animatedly, hands waving

while she alternates between talking and eating, and how Rory watches her, listening and nodding in all the right places. He asks questions about her games of play-pretend with the same intensity and care that he does when Sloan is talking about Black Rose business.

It's sweet as fuck, and it makes me realize there's a lot more to this guy than just dedication to his gang. There's at least one other thing in the world that's as important to him as that organization, and I'm looking at her right now.

Once we're all done, he clears away the bowls and shoos Piper into the living room for a second while he puts everything in the sink.

She's sitting on the couch with the TV remote in her hand when we emerge from the kitchen, eyes big.

"Oh, god." Rory groans. "Again?"

"Please, Daddy?" she asks, poking out her lower lip. "It's my favorite."

He sighs heavily, but I can tell it's half faked for humor. "She wants to watch this princess movie," he explains to me, dropping down onto the couch and then patting the spot beside him. Piper clambers over to sit in his lap, and I'm startled to realize he's patting that spot for me.

I only hesitate for a second before dropping down to sit next to him, keeping some distance between us. I don't like the way my heart is racing, or the way I can't stop looking at him, and if I had my way, I would've sat in the chair on the other side of the end table, but I don't want to cause a scene in front of Piper.

The little girl smiles at me and then goes back to trying to convince her father to put on her favorite movie.

"Tell him!" she says to me all of a sudden, and I blink, realizing I definitely missed whatever I'm supposed to be telling Rory.

"You should listen to her," I say, hoping that will cover it.

Rory gives me a look like he knows I have no idea what's going on, but he sighs and takes the remote from Piper. "I can tell when I'm outnumbered. Princess Parade it is." He glances at me once more and smirks. "You are going to regret this."

I roll my eyes at him. "Not scared of you."

"Oh, I don't mean me. Just wait."

He puts the movie on, and Piper settles in against him, watching the screen eagerly. It only takes a few minutes for Rory's words to start making sense. The Princess Parade movie is... really fucking bad.

The plot makes no sense as far as I can tell. There seem to be a bunch of random princesses trying to put on a parade to celebrate... being princesses, I guess? I don't know. There's a musical number every five minutes or so, and no one in the movie can sing at all. Piper sounds better than they do when she sings along, and when I cringe at the flat notes, Rory grins at me triumphantly.

I just about remember not to flip him off in front of his daughter, but it's an excruciating hour and ten minutes before the movie is over.

"Sometimes," Rory whispers. "She makes me watch it twice."

I shudder just thinking about it, and luckily, Piper doesn't want to watch the movie again once the credits roll. Instead she declares that she wants to play blocks, which is a relief.

Rory goes to fetch the blocks in question, and Piper eyes me a bit. "Play?" she asks, and I smile at her, hoping it's an acceptable one.

"Sure. I love blocks."

I haven't played with blocks since I was a kid myself and my dad brought home a beat up box filled with all kinds of blocks that he found at a thrift shop. They were all different shapes and sizes and looked like someone had just dumped all the toys their kid had outgrown into a box and donated it, but I loved them.

Piper seems to have the same enthusiasm for her toys, because she practically throws herself on the floor in front of her blocks and starts stacking them into an elaborate configuration. After a second, she glances up at me expectantly, and I hurry to join her, smiling as I settle in.

They're bigger than Legos, probably so she can't accidentally swallow one, and I start constructing a tower beside the structure she's making.

She babbles happily to me while we build things, and it's actually pretty fun. I haven't ever spent that much time around kids, but she's really sweet and seems to be having a good time, so it's easier than I thought it would be. I answer her questions as best I can, and through the whole thing I can feel Rory's eyes on me from where he sits on the couch, but I don't turn around to look at him.

After another hour or so, Jen comes back, sweeping into the house with a grin, still singing some song from the radio. She takes one look at Piper and me on the floor with the blocks, and I half expect her to take Rory to task for letting some stranger play with their daughter.

But instead, she just tosses her purse on the couch and gets down to play with us.

"Rory's too good for blocks," she says, voice lowered like she's sharing a secret between the three of us. "Look at him sitting there on the couch like he's too good to build things. It's not like the floor's dirty. Who does he think he is?"

I laugh, and Piper giggles, glancing up at her dad to shake her head.

Rory just grins and leans back, arms spread out against the back of the couch. "Why would I want to be down there on the floor when I've got the best view from up here? Three lovely ladies being creative? Nothing beats it."

Jen rolls her eyes and tosses a block at him, and he catches it in midair which is... something. He just grins and tosses it back into the pile, knocking over Jen's blocky house in the process.

"Oops," he says, sounding anything but sorry.

"One of these days, I'm going to make you pay for that," she says. "You won't know when, and you won't know how, but it's going to happen."

"You've been saying that for four years, Jen," Rory replies. "And I'm still in one piece."

"For now."

It's the kind of playful banter that Scarlett and I have when we're just hanging out, and it's funny and interesting to see. Rory clearly spends a lot of time here, and he seems just as comfortable bickering with the mother of his child and playing with Piper as he does doing anything I've ever seen him do. He doesn't even seem to mind doing it in front of me, which is still kind of surprising.

It's something I would have thought he'd want to keep private, especially since he keeps Black Rose business separate from his family, and I'm pretty sure I fall into the category of Black Rose business.

But it's not awkward, and Jen and Piper seem happy enough to have me there.

Once it starts getting closer to dinner time, Jen gets up and brushes herself off. "I should get dinner going," she says, cracking her back in a stretch. "Are you two hanging around?"

I glance at Rory who shakes his head. "Nah, we should

be getting back. It's my turn to cook at the house, and Levi and Sloan might burn the kitchen down without me there."

He gets up, and I follow his lead, heading for the door while he hugs Jen and scoops Piper up to smother her face in kisses. She giggles and reaches up to pat his cheeks with her chubby hands. "Bye, Daddy."

"Bye, kiddo. I'll see you soon, okay?"

She nods, and he passes her to Jen, who waves at me before we head out.

It's a short walk back to his car and my bike, and I glance at Rory periodically, trying to reconcile all the things I know about him now with the things I knew before. When I set out to follow him today, the last thing I thought I'd find out was that he has a kid. I was expecting all kinds of sinister shit, and I don't quite know what to do with the reality.

We split up to head back home, and I follow him more closely on my bike this time since I'm not trying to stay off his radar. When we pull up outside the house, he gets out of his car and waits for me while I climb off my bike. He's leaning against the driver's side door, arms crossed as he watches me. He makes no move to head toward the front door, and I stuff my hands in my pockets, coming to stand in front of him.

"Piper's a sweet kid," I offer, not sure what else to say.

"She is," he agrees. "She likes you."

I don't know how to respond to that, so I don't say anything. He doesn't move, flicking a glance at my bike before looking back at me.

"So," he says, and it's obvious he's been waiting to bring this up. "Why were you following me? What were you hoping to find?"

That serious look is back on his face, and I waffle a bit. I really don't want to admit that I was hoping following him would lead me to some dirt on the Black Rose gang that I could use against them. I may not be the best spy in the world, but even *I* know that would be a very bad idea.

I could make excuses or come up with a lie, but instead, I let my mind settle on the urge I've had since I first saw him with Piper in his arms.

I give in to it, taking a step forward and leaning up to kiss him right on the mouth.

There's a second of surprise on his part. I can feel it in the way he stiffens under my touch. But then he's kissing me back, one hand going around the back of my neck to pull me in closer. His fingers tangle in my hair, which is windblown from riding the bike, and he bends me backward a little as he deepens the kiss.

I wrap my arms around him, letting my fingers play over the broad muscles of his back through his soft t-shirt. As our tongues slide against each other, he pulls me closer against his body. His hands stray down my back and come just shy of cupping my ass, a slow tease that has him grinning against my lips when I make an impatient noise.

As always, it's so easy to get distracted by these men. I only wanted to change the subject, and now here I am, lost in his fucking kiss and wanting him to touch me more.

"You're trouble, did you know that, Hurricane?" he murmurs, his warm breath ghosting over my lips.

He's not the first person to say that about me, and I'm sure he won't be the last.

But the truth is, he's trouble too.

19

I'M NOT sure what the reason is, but over the next few days, the guys start to be a little more lax in their watch over me. They're wrapped up in their own shit, busy and distracted, and they don't seem to care what I do all that much.

Maybe it's them starting to trust me, and I can't help but think about Rory and how I followed him.

He could've been furious at me for following him, especially since he seems to keep Piper and Jen separate from his work shit. But instead, he invited me in. He trusted me with his family, and maybe that was the beginning of him trusting me more in general.

No matter what the cause, I plan to take advantage of it. If they give me more freedom of movement, maybe I can get a chance to listen in on more conversations like the one

I heard at the training gym. Maybe I can leave the house more without them tracking my every damn move.

Testing my theory that I've become more like a fourth roommate than a complete prisoner, I invite Scarlett to come over one afternoon after school, not telling the guys until the last minute.

They're all gathered in the kitchen, talking and drinking coffee while Rory makes sandwiches for lunch, and I walk in, stepping past Sloan to open the fridge and take out a bottle of water.

"Oh," I say, going for casual. "Scarlett's coming over later."

I keep my back to them, pretending to rummage in the fridge for something else while I wait for their answer.

"Okay," Levi says, sounding like he doesn't care one way or any another.

"Two beautiful ladies in the house?" Rory asks, and I don't need to see his face to know he's got some smug smile on it. "Be still my heart."

I roll my eyes at that.

Sloan just grunts, and I take that to mean he doesn't care either and emerge from the fridge with my water bottle in hand. The whole conversation definitely goes easier than I thought it would, and I take that to mean my freedoms are more open than they were before.

The doorbell rings half an hour later, and I go to answer the door before one of the guys can get to it.

"Hey, hot stuff." Scarlett grins and throws herself at me in a hug.

"Hey, Scar."

I bury my face in her hair for a second, pleased as always to smell the familiar scent of her shampoo. She's been using the same one since we were in high school, something inexpensive that makes her hair soft and floral-scented, and it always makes me feel close to her when I smell it. With my dad still out of the picture for the time being, having Scarlett with me is the next best thing.

I let her in, and she follows the sound of voices to the living room where the guys have moved.

"Well, if it isn't my three favorite gang members," she says brightly, greeting the men when we walk in.

They're sprawled across the furniture carelessly, flipping through the channels on the TV. She's only met them a couple of times, but that doesn't stop her from talking to them like she knows them well. She knows more about them than they know about her, just from hearing me bitch about them so much, probably.

Scarlett gives a low whistle as she glances around the living room, and I remember she's never been at the house before. I've described it to her a little, but I'm not sure I did it justice.

"Damn." She shakes her head. "You know, Mercy, when you told me you got kidnapped by Black Rose members, I didn't think that meant you were living in the lap of luxury. This place is fucking huge."

"Kidnapped is a strong word," Rory chimes in, flashing his crookedly charming smile at Scarlett.

She doesn't blush, but it's a close thing, and I can see her eyeing all three of them up as they lounge comfortably. They're sexy as fuck, and we both know it. Hopefully she won't start going on about it right here in front of them.

"You literally grabbed me and put me in a car against my will," I argue. "That's like the textbook definition of kidnapping."

Levi snorts and shakes his head. "We don't treat you badly though."

"That's beside the point."

"I sort of pictured them keeping you in a basement somewhere," Scarlett says. "Or like one of those houses that looks like a crack den from the outside. I definitely didn't think it would be like this."

I roll my eyes. We've talked and texted enough times that she knew I wasn't being kept in a basement. If I were, she probably would've stormed this place weeks ago, determined to bust me out no matter what happened.

But she has a point. Their obnoxious attitudes and hard-to-resist faces aside, the guys have treated me pretty well. I eat well, have my own room and bathroom, and they don't ask me to cook and clean or anything. Unless they're in shitty moods, they mostly leave me to my own devices these days.

It's something to be grateful for, but I feel weird about trusting it. My dad is still out there, doing whatever dirty work they pushed on him, and I'm here, sometimes eating crepes on Sunday mornings when Rory's feeling fancy.

It's weird.

Scarlett isn't intimidated by any of the guys, which makes me love her even more than I already do. Sloan is standoffish and curt when he deigns to speak at all, but she doesn't bat an eyelash, continuing on with whatever she's saying.

It's more comfortable than I would have expected it to be.

"Don't let her fool you," Levi says, looking away from the TV. "We're not that bad."

Scarlett hums, tapping a finger against her lips. "Maybe, but the last time I saw you guys, you were carting Mercy out of the bar in some macho, alpha male display of power, so I'm not sure that counts as being *good* either."

Sloan makes a face. "There was nothing 'macho' about it," he mutters. "It was necessary."

I just roll my eyes and refuse to get into that with him. I'm still pretending most of that night never happened. "We're going out," I say, making the decision on the spot. "I need some air."

"Fine," Sloan replies, waving a hand. "Go."

Neither of the other two argue, and Rory waggles his fingers in a little wave as I go to get my shoes on and grab my purse, Scarlett hot on my heels.

I haven't been out without them in so long that it feels weird to leave the house without one or all of them shadowing me, and I breathe a sigh of relief when I get in Scarlett's car, leaning back and closing my eyes as she pulls out of the driveway.

"So where do you want to go with this newfound freedom?" she asks, glancing over at me.

"I don't know, anywhere. Let's get coffee."

Scarlett nods, and we head for the little coffee shop not far from campus where we used to hang out all the time before everything went to hell. She parks, and we get out. As we walk into the small shop, I'm immediately comforted by the smell of roasted coffee beans and the familiar sound of people chattering as they sit with their drinks.

It's been too long since I was able to just be out without having to worry about the guys breathing down my neck, and I order a large iced coffee and go to snag us a table near the front windows.

"Okay. Talk to me," Scarlett says, plonking down into the seat opposite mine when she has her drink as well. "What's been going on?"

We've seen each other on campus over the past week,

but only briefly and always with Levi present, so we haven't had a chance to really talk.

I open my mouth to tell her, but then close it again. Because where do I begin, honestly? It hasn't been that long since the guys were dragging me out of Sapphire, but it feels like so much has happened. I lick my lips and take another sip of my drink.

"A lot, actually. So. I haven't exactly been as careful as I should have been."

It feels weird to admit that out loud, but Scarlett is my best friend and the one person I tell everything to. I can't keep it from her, and honestly, I want to get it off my chest.

"What do you mean?" she asks, leaning over the table so she's closer to me. "Have you been..." She waggles her eyebrows, and I don't need her to elaborate to know what she's getting at.

"Yeah, I guess so. There have been some... developments."

Her eyes light up, and she has her fingers in a stranglehold around her cup. "Tell me! I need the details."

"Okay, okay," I say, gesturing for her to keep her voice down. "You know I hooked up with Levi, right? A year ago?" She nods. "Well, I thought that was that, but apparently he wanted more. And I know this because he burst into my room after we got back from being out and kissed me."

"After they dragged you out of the club?"

"Same night, but we went somewhere else after that." I fill her in about the training gym and the fight I got into and how pissed Sloan got. "He punched out the guy I was fighting in one hit and then stalked me to the locker room where I went to go cool off."

"Mercy DeLeon, did you fuck him in a locker room?" Scar asks, wide eyed.

"No!" I shake my head vigorously, then bite my bottom lip. "I mean. We didn't fuck. He just. He ate me out. While I was bent over the sink."

She squeals, making a couple of people sitting close to us look over curiously. I kick her under the table, and she sighs.

"Sorry, sorry." She holds up her hands. "I just... I can't believe it. I can't believe it was *Sloan*, of all people, either. He's so... broody."

"Yeah." I snort. "And irritable. Anyway, that happened, and then Levi walked in before we could go any further."

I still don't know if I'm relieved or disappointed about the interruption, but it's best not to dwell on it, I figure. I'm not sure I would be happy with what I discovered if I thought too hard about how I feel about that night.

Scar nods, her eyes still wide. "And that's why he kissed you after you got home? Levi?"

"Yeah. Well. I also kissed Rory after the Sloan thing, but that was just to prove a point."

"You *what?*"

"I mean, it wasn't the first time."

Her eyebrows shoot up even higher, and she blinks twice, then shakes her head. "Whoa, whoa, whoa. Okay, hot stuff, I'm gonna need you to start from the beginning. How many times have you kissed these guys?"

I take another long sip of my coffee and try to get my thoughts in order, starting from the beginning. Levi and I hooked up a year ago, there was the kiss with Rory in the home gym, and then the whole mess with them at the training gym. Kissing Rory after meeting his family too.

By the time I finish laying it all out for her, I want to kick myself for being so fucking reckless, especially considering how I promised Scarlett I would be careful around them.

"Holy shit, Mercy. It's like you're building a harem or something," she says when I stop speaking. "A harem of hot, dangerous men who seem to be especially attracted to you." She lets out a breath that's almost a wistful sigh.

"I didn't ask for this," I remind her, jamming my straw into the cup and swirling the ice around. "And it's not a harem. It's just... I don't know. Three guys who drive me fucking nuts."

"In a good way, it sounds like. I know they're assholes for what they're doing, but it seems like they like you. And I think you like them more than you want to admit." Scarlett tips her head to the side. "I guess since you're a girl, it would be more like a reverse harem."

"That's not a thing, Scar," I tell her, knowing it's probably pointless to argue about it.

"Sure it is. And if it's not, then you're just a pioneer. And I mean, it could be worse. They could be three *ugly* guys keeping you at their place."

In spite of myself, I laugh. "Trust you to have your priorities in the right order," I tease her, shaking my head. She's right, but in a way it would be easier if they weren't so damn attractive. At least then I could keep my focus better.

"Hey, I'm just trying to help you see the good spots in all of this. It's the kind of situation where you could use a silver lining," Scarlett points out. She props her chin up on her hand and gives me a look. "How's your dad doing?"

That takes most of the teasing out of the conversation, and things turn serious. I keep swirling the ice in my cup, swallowing around the sudden lump in my throat.

In a way, I feel almost ashamed to admit I don't know. I'm his daughter, all he has left, and there's nothing I can do to help him beyond trying to dig up some kind of dirt on the men holding me as collateral. I don't even know where he is or if he's safe.

I glance up at Scarlett, and I know she can read all of that on my face.

"I just... I hope this works," I tell her, my voice strained. "This bargain. Because they were going to kill him, Scarlett. They were ready to kill him that night, and they won't give him another chance."

She nods, looking solemn. "It's a bad place to be. But he's strong. He can do whatever it is they want him to do, right?"

"Probably? I mean, I have no idea what they want from him. And even if he does it, how do I know it's not just delaying the inevitable, you know? How do I know this will be the end of it? It might go badly no matter what."

Scarlett reaches over and pats my hand, and we finish our drinks and head back out. The ride back to the house is quiet, and I'm lost in thought when we pull up out front.

"Hey," Scarlett says, reaching over to poke me in the shoulder. "It'll be okay. I believe that. One way or another."

I muster a smile for her. "Thanks, Scar. What would I do without you?"

"Oh, probably suffer and die horribly," she shoots back, grinning and getting out of the car when I do. She pulls me into a big hug, and I bury my face in the crook of her neck for a second, taking comfort in her warmth and her smell. No matter what changes or goes to hell around me, Scarlett has always been there. Always been steady and constant. I hope to god she always will be.

I let go and wave when she gets back in her car to drive off, and then head inside the house. I can hear the guys talking loudly in the living room, and I walk through, intending to head up to my room and maybe take a nap or a bath or something. Something to get my mind off of the conversation about my dad and my worries.

"Hey, Hurricane!" Rory calls before I can get very far, his head popping up over the back of the couch. "Come here."

I frown at him for being bossy, but I turn and make my way over. There's some action movie on the screen, a car chase playing out with the music thumping through the surround sound speakers. There are beers and liquor bottles on the coffee table, and it's clear the guys have had more than a couple of drinks already.

"Come hang out with us," Rory says, giving me big puppy eyes.

I laugh and shake my head. "Nah, I'm just going to head upstairs. I'm tired."

"Mercy," Levi chimes in. "Come on. You spend so much time upstairs already."

I bite back the comment about how maybe that's their fault and glance at Sloan. He's looking back at me, and for once, he's not scowling.

Before I can make a decision either way, Rory grabs my arm and pulls me down onto the couch between him and Sloan. I should tell him off for not listening to me, but the couch is comfortable, and watching a movie with them is probably better than spending the night in my room alone. *Probably.*

Rory leans forward and snags a beer from the table and holds it out to me, wiggling it teasingly. I roll my eyes and snatch it up, making a show of using the edge of the coffee table to pop the cap off in a practiced gesture.

Levi laughs and Rory pretends to swoon. There's even a little smile on Sloan's face as we settle in to watch.

It's a terrible movie, with bad effects and even worse acting. The car chase goes on for another twenty minutes, and Levi throws his bottle cap at the screen. "Catch this asshole already!" He snorts. "So we don't have to watch you pretend to drive anymore." He jerks an invisible steering wheel wildly to the left and right, imitating the main hero of the movie.

"It's not about the driving," Sloan says. "It's about the car."

"It's not even that nice of a car," I put in. "And it would be way more banged up if it was jumping over medians and shit like that."

"She's right," Levi agrees, pointing at me. "She's so right."

"You're so drunk," Rory accuses with a laugh.

Levi flips him off and takes a pointed swig of his beer at the same time. I sip mine, keeping my eyes on the screen and not the way Levi's mouth looks against the bottle.

The car chase finally ends, and the hero ends up crashing into a pond in the middle of a public park, which sparks more jeering from the guys and laughter from me.

The next scene has him walking up the stairs to an apartment building, and the music goes low and sultry. "Enter... the love interest," Rory drawls, making his voice all breathy and soft.

He's not wrong, and a blonde woman with huge tits wearing a bathrobe comes to the door.

"It's four in the afternoon." I frown, making a face. "Why is she in a bathrobe?"

"It's called depression, Mercy," Rory shoots back. "And I'd be depressed too if I was dating someone that bad at driving."

"You *are* that bad at driving," Sloan mutters from my other side. Rory misses it, but I smother a laugh.

It keeps going like that, the three of them giving each other shit and yelling at the screen as the movie goes on, and eventually I yawn and settle in to watch them watch the movie, letting my own comments drop out.

Before I know it, my eyes are closing, and I put my empty beer bottle on the table, deciding not to fight it.

I have no idea how much time passes, but when I open my eyes again, the screen is paused on the scrolling credits, and I blink blearily.

My head is pillowed on a strong chest, the soft material of a well-worn t-shirt under the skin of my cheek. I yawn and stretch a bit, trying to get my bearings while rubbing at my eyes with one hand. When it finally makes it through my tired brain that I've been sleeping on one of them, I stiffen and sit up quickly, cheeks immediately going pink in embarrassment.

It's Sloan, because of *course* it's Sloan.

If it was Rory, there would be some flirtatious teasing and that would be the end of it, but Sloan looks stiff and tense, and when I glance at his face, it's unreadable.

For once, he doesn't look like he's a second away from punching a hole in a wall, but it's clear he's acting like nothing happened, like he doesn't give a shit.

His eyes meet mine for all of a second, and then he's back to staring at the TV again. He's playing it cool, and he doesn't say anything, but the fact remains that he let me curl up like that. He didn't move me off of him while I was sleeping. Given how easily he's been pushing me around and grabbing me when he wants to, if he didn't want me there, he could have just pushed me off with no issue.

Instead of bringing any of that up, I yawn and stretch and get to my feet, hurrying up the stairs so I can curl up in my own bed and stop thinking about how broad and warm Sloan's chest is.

I change into a comfy tank top and get under the covers, and it's not hard to recapture that feeling of comfort and warmth that lulls me back to sleep easily enough. Just as I'm drifting off, I realize I can still smell him. That sharp, woodsy scent settles around me, clinging to me and now my sheets. I catch myself inhaling it deeply for a second, and then I frown.

Goddammit. Why is that smell so fucking addictive?

Why is *he*?

A FEW MORE DAYS PASS, and it's almost weird how routine things have become. It was once so strange to be here, in their house, being trailed around by them whenever I wanted to do anything, but now it's just mundane. It's become a part of my life, and I can't tell if I should be worried about that or not.

On Friday, I step out of my last class of the day with a relieved sigh. It's been a long week, and I'm tired and ready for the weekend, even if all I manage to accomplish is doing some laundry and lying around. Maybe I'll invite Scarlett over and we can have a movie night of our own, watching the rom-coms that are a guilty pleasure for me, and some of Scarlett's favorites, with a few action films thrown in for good measure.

I've also been poking around the house a little more, careful not to draw attention to myself. It's not like the guys are leaving important Black Rose memos all over the place, but I'm sure there's gotta be some shit worth getting into somewhere in the massive house. I just need to find it.

When I leave the building where my class is held, Levi's in his usual spot against the wall, arms folded, but he pushes off and grins at me when I walk over to him. I wait to see if he's going to explain what he's smiling about, but he doesn't say anything.

I roll my eyes. "What are you so excited about? If being cooped up on my campus day in and day out bothers you so much that you're literally giddy with joy at the end of the day, you could always just stop coming with me."

He shakes his head and then rolls his eyes in turn. "That's not it."

"Then what?"

"It's a surprise," he says, his grin turning teasing. "You'll just have to wait and see."

There was definitely a time when hearing that Levi or either of the other two had a surprise for me would make me immediately worried about what it was. But now I just feel curious, wondering what they're all up to—because I don't believe for a second that this is all Levi's doing.

We walk back to the car and head home, and Levi just keeps smiling until I head upstairs to my room.

There, draped across the bed, is probably the sexiest, most elegant dress I've ever seen outside of like a magazine or the internet. It's fiery red and long, probably almost floor length on me. The halter style neckline plunges low, designed to show off a lot of cleavage in the front and pretty much all of the back from what I can tell when I hold it up. It's definitely not meant to be worn with a bra.

The material is silky and smooth in my hands when I touch it, except for a line of delicate beading along the waist that shimmers in the light.

It's beautiful.

And I'm immediately suspicious.

I fold the dress over one arm and head back down the stairs to the kitchen where Sloan and Levi are talking.

"So what the fuck is this all about?" I ask, gesturing to the pile of fabric over my arm.

I expect Levi to finally come clean about whatever he's been so smug about, but it's Sloan who answers me, much to my surprise.

"There's a party this weekend," he says. "We're all going, and you're coming with us. We thought you might need something to wear."

He casts a glance up and down my jeans and t-shirt, and I narrow my eyes at him.

"Are you sure you want me to come?" I ask him. "After the last time you guys took me out, you didn't seem to approve of my behavior." I let my voice go dry and sarcastic, so there's no way he can miss just how I feel about that.

He narrows his eyes right back at me, heat springing into those storm gray depths.

"Then you'll just have to be on your best behavior this time, won't you?" he asks, and it's not teasing even a little. It's like he's almost daring me to piss him off at this party, to give him another excuse to haul me into a room alone.

And fuck. I've been doing so well at not thinking about that, not giving him the satisfaction of knowing how fucking hot it still is that we did that. Even standing right there, I can feel that clench in my core, the desperate pull that makes me really want to test him, just to see what he's going to do about it.

My tongue darts out to lick my lips, and I watch his gaze follow the motion, willing myself not to blush and give my own arousal away.

"I know I say this so much I sound like a broken record at this point," I say, putting my free hand on my hip. "But you're not the boss of me. I can do what I want."

Before he can reply, I turn on my heel and go back upstairs with the dress, heart racing just a little.

As annoyed as I am by Sloan, I have to admit—to myself in my own head—that I'm looking forward to this party a little bit. For one thing, it'll be with other Black Rose members, more than likely, which will give me another chance to learn about the organization and what they might be up to. Ever since I followed Rory to Jen's house last weekend, my information gathering hasn't gone anywhere, and this is a chance to fix that.

For another thing, I'm still a bit stir-crazy. I like the idea of going out, and looking nice while doing it.

THE NEXT NIGHT, the guys tell me to be ready by eight, and they disappear into their rooms to get ready while I do the same. I shower and shave and even take the time to put on some makeup and curl my hair.

If I'm going to be wearing a gorgeous dress, then the rest of me might as well match it, I figure. I don't get dressed up often, but the few occasions that call for it seem to be a good chance to go all-out.

I line my eyes with liner and a little gold sparkle, making them pop and really bringing out how green they are. My lipstick matches the dress, bright red and killer. I leave my hair loose, letting it fall over my shoulders in soft dark curls that I pin back on one side to keep out of my face.

The dress feels good on me when I step into it, and of course it fits perfectly. I have no idea where the guys got it, or how they guessed my measurements so accurately, but I'm not complaining. It's comfortable and beautiful, and when I move to go put shoes on, I realize there's a slit up the side that goes all the way to my thigh, showing a lot of leg.

Grabbing my phone, I head out of my room. I feel sexy

as hell as I walk down the stairs later, the dress moving around my ankles as I do.

The guys are already gathered in the living room, talking in low voices, and I get a good look at them before they see me. Of course they look fucking amazing. I haven't seen any one of them look bad in anything yet.

Like when we went to Sapphire a couple weeks ago, they're dressed in casual, but nice outfits, clearly designed to show off how well built they all are.

Levi and Sloan are in dark colors, black slacks and a black shirt for Sloan, the sleeves not rolled up this time, but the top two buttons of his shirt undone, showing skin there that my gaze immediately goes to. Levi's shirt is a rich gray with a slight pattern to it, tucked into his black slacks. It shows off the spread of his shoulders and the trimness of his waist.

Rory's the only one other than me who isn't mono-chrome tonight, and his blue shirt makes his green eyes seem even brighter than normal and sets off the golden tones in his hair.

He's the first one to see me as I come down, and he stops mid-sentence to stare at me. "Holy shit," he murmurs.

The other two turn to look, and I fight the urge to blush as all three of them ogle me a little, taking me in from head to toe, paying special attention to the flash of thigh seen through the slit in my dress.

Rory comes over and gives a low whistle and then drags a knuckle down my bare arm, setting off goosebumps in the wake of his touch.

"We did a good job," Levi says.

"Oh sure, give yourselves all the credit," I reply, making a face.

"We picked out the dress." Rory grins down at me, heat warming his green irises. "But you really bring it to life. Let's call it a team effort, shall we?"

My lips twitch in a smile, and I roll my eyes and shrug. "Whatever. Are we going?"

"We're going," Sloan confirms, taking the lead toward the door without a backward look. Levi moves to follow him, but not before letting his fingers brush against the small of my back, the feeling a little electric since my back is basically bare in this dress.

Rory does a gallant "after you" bow, and I fall in line, feeling the burn of his gaze as he checks out my ass and the curve of my back while we walk.

For once, I don't even really mind all that much.

The easy, light mood carries over as we drive to the party, and we pull up to a large house on the edge of town. It's twice as big as the one the guys live in, with a sloped driveway and manicured lawns. Lights twinkle from the windows, and even though it's a fancy place, the music playing is the low, thumping kind that I associate with house parties at much less nice houses.

These are gang members, after all. They can dress up nice and live in mansions or whatever, but they still know how to get down.

The place is already pretty packed when we get in, and I can feel eyes on me as we push through the crowd of people to one of the center rooms. There's a woman standing behind a wet bar, twirling bottles as she pours some into a shaker for the amusement of the people waiting for their drinks.

Unlike at Sapphire, the guys don't seem to want to peel off on their own to hang around on the fringes looking menacing. They stay around me, forming almost a triangle of protection as we make our way over to the bar.

"What do you want?" Levi asks. He has to lean in for me to hear him over the music and chatter, and his breath brushes against my ear as he does.

I swallow hard, trying to keep it together and not get all melty five minutes into this party.

"Whiskey sour," I say, thinking about one of my dad's favorite drinks.

He gives me a look that's a little impressed, and I flash him a smile as he steps up to get drinks for us.

Sloan moves to take his spot, not saying a word to me but staying close. Anyone who seems like they want to come talk to me takes one look at him and suddenly they have somewhere else to be.

It would be annoying as hell if it didn't feel like... well, like they're trying to protect me. I don't know any of the other Black Rose members, can't say what kind of people they are or what they might want, and it's clear Levi, Sloan, and Rory want to keep an eye on me.

Levi comes back with drinks, and he hands me mine with a little wink. I take a sip, and the whiskey burns against the tartness of the lemon, but it's good. Strong and sour and it reminds me of my dad.

Rory laughs and leans a bit closer into my side with his own glass in hand, something clear and fizzy with a lime shoved in the glass. "Gorgeous and you can hold your liquor," he teases. "What can't you do?"

He's close enough that I can feel the heat of his body against my bare arm, and that plus the drink brings a slight flush to my face that hopefully will go unnoticed in the dim light of the room.

The song changes while we stand in a tight knot, and I watch Sloan knock back whatever he's drinking with one smooth swallow. He glances over, catching my look, and then tips his head in the direction of my half empty glass like he's asking if I want another one.

There's a little challenge in it, the way there always is when it comes to Sloan, and I follow his lead, finishing off the first drink and nodding at him to get me another.

He doesn't smile because he's Sloan and I'm convinced he doesn't really know how, but he does nod back and move through the crush of people to get to the bar once more.

"What is this party for?" I ask Levi, stepping a bit closer to him to let a group of women go past us.

He shrugs his shoulder. "Nothing in particular. We just like to unwind every once in a while."

I can't tell if he's being cagey about what it's actually for, or if the Black Roses truly just decide to throw nice parties every now and then. Everyone seems relaxed, drinking and talking, disappearing up the stairs and into other rooms to do who knows what.

Gavin Kennedy isn't here tonight, or at least, I haven't seen him. Just like the night at the warehouse, this gathering seems to be primarily for the younger members of the gang. There's no tension in the air like someone's spoiling for a fight, and no one's talking about hunting down members of the Jackals or anything, so maybe it *is* just a chill party to relax and have fun.

That's definitely how the guys seem to be taking it. Sloan comes back with two drinks in hand, and he passes mine to me, the same whiskey sour as before.

"Thanks," I murmur. Our hands brush a little when I reach to take the drink from him. A spark of electricity jumps between us, but Sloan turns away before I can tell if he feels it too.

"Hey. Sloan, there you are," a tall man with a neat beard says as he comes over. "I need to talk to you."

Sloan nods and glances back at Rory and Levi for a second before following the man off to some remote corner of the party so they can talk business or whatever.

It's not long before someone comes and does the same to Rory, roping him into an impassioned conversation as the two of them drift away into the crowd.

"Black Rose business calls, I guess," I murmur, and Levi nods.

"That's usually how it is. Whenever we're all together, we take the opportunity to check in."

I open my mouth to ask him what they're checking in about, but before the words come out, someone steps up to Levi and launches into a low voiced rant. Levi glances at me and then leads the man away, leaving me standing alone.

I consider dancing or trying to mingle, but I feel very outnumbered. I don't know any of these people except the three I came with, and I'm not stupid enough to think I can trust them.

I don't know what they're involved in or who knows about my dad, and I don't want to end up dancing with the wrong person or something. So I stay put, sipping my drink slowly and trying to tune into the cacophony of multiple conversations all happening at once around me.

All three of the guys I came with have stepped away to talk business, and none of them are close enough for me to listen in on them without being obvious. But maybe I can do some snooping on other people.

Music blares through the room, making it even harder to eavesdrop, but I tilt my head a little to one side as I listen to a few people converse to my left.

When my phone buzzes in my hand, the vibration against my palm startles me. I flip it over and see my dad's picture flash on the screen.

Holy shit.

My heart races, and I immediately put my drink down and step outside to answer it. I haven't heard from him since they took him away to do whatever they want him to do, and I have to know if he's all right. On top of that, I just really, really want to hear his voice.

"Dad?" I say, hitting the button to answer the call as soon as I'm outside and can hear. "Dad, are you okay?"

"Hey, kiddo," he replies. "It's good to hear your voice."

It doesn't slip past me that he doesn't answer the question, and he sounds tired. I've heard exhaustion in his voice before. Being a single parent wasn't always easy for him, and there were definitely days that wore him down more than others. But this sounds like a new kind of tired. One that might be born from fear, and it kicks my anxiety up a notch.

"How are things going?" I ask.

"Fine." He hesitates for a beat. "As fine as they can be. How are you? Are they treating you okay?"

"Yeah." I nod, even though he can't see me, gripping the phone tightly. I don't want him worrying about me. "It's all fine. I'm still going to classes and everything."

"Good," he says, then sighs. "That's good. I'd hate for you to be suffering because of something I fucked up. I always wanted the best for you, you know that, right? I just want you to be happy and okay."

"Dad," I cut it. "What's going on? You're talking like..."

Like he's worried he's not going to see me again and doesn't want to say it.

He sighs again, a heavy sound. "It's fine, Mercy, I promise. There's... a lot going on. I'm running out of time, and I'm not sure I can..." He trails off as if he doesn't want to finish that thought. When he speaks again, something in his tone has shifted. "But you don't need to worry, okay, kiddo? Not about me."

That's asking for a hell of a lot, all things considered. He's all I have left, and every day that I don't hear from him and don't know what's going on makes it harder to be sure he's going to come back.

I've spent the past several weeks trying to find a sense of purpose in all of this, some goal to cling to that would help keep me from going insane with worry. I've been trying to keep it together, to find some semblance of normalcy and equilibrium in the fucked up new path my life has taken.

But hearing my dad's voice—and the fear and defeat in it—makes all of the illusions come crashing down.

I can tell he's trying to be strong, that he wants to seem like he has it all together, but I know him. I've known him my whole life, and I can always tell when he's pretending, trying to downplay things so I don't get concerned or scared.

"You just keep taking care of yourself," he says quietly, his voice rough. "I know you're tough and you're smart, and I know you're not going to let anything get you down. You don't have to worry about me."

My heart jolts. The more adamantly he insists I shouldn't worry, the more certain I am that I *should* worry.

"Dad, I—"

"I love you, Mercy. So much. I gotta go."

Before I can get another word in, he hangs up, leaving me standing outside in the cool night air with the phone pressed to my ear.

For a second, all I feel is a creeping sort of numbness.

There's no way of knowing what's really going on, and it paralyzes me for a second. And then the freak out starts, the fear and worry rising in me like nausea, threatening to overflow.

This is it. This is it, and I don't know what to do. My dad, my best friend for so long, the man who raised me and sacrificed and gave everything I have, is going to die.

There's nothing I can do to stop it, and whatever this assignment Sloan's dad gave him is going to get him killed.

I stand stock still for a second, gripping my phone tightly as I replay every word of the conversation over in my head.

My dad sounded like someone who was afraid for their life. Like he wanted to check in and make sure I was okay so he'd know that I was taken care of no matter what happens.

No matter if he comes back to me or not.

It's unbearable, and it makes tears burn the backs of my eyes. I could tell from his voice that he felt like he let me down, but the truth is, I let *him* down. I should've been able to find a way to leverage my position at the guys' house by now. If I'd gotten hold of something damaging to use against them, maybe I could've struck a bargain in exchange for Dad's release from whatever "favor" he owes them.

But I didn't uncover enough. And now it's too late.

I turn on my heel and quickly march back inside. I need one of the guys. One of them, all of them. They have to know what's happening. They have to be able to do something.

Almost mindlessly, I push through the bodies in the middle of the room we were in before. Some people give me looks of annoyance, but I ignore them, continuing to shove my way through until I spot Levi standing in a cluster of guys having a conversation.

"Levi," I breathe and grab his arm, trying to tug him away.

His brow furrows as he looks at me. "Hey. Is everything okay?"

"I need to talk to you," I tell him, and whatever he sees in my face makes him nod and excuse himself from the conversation. I pull him over to a relatively quiet corner and wrap my arms around myself.

"What's going on, Mercy?" he asks me, frowning.

"I need—you have to find a way to let my dad out of this bargain."

"What?"

"Whatever it is he's doing, he can't." My stomach feels like it's twisting itself into a giant knot, making the drinks I had earlier slosh around unpleasantly. "It's going to kill him, and you have to do something."

Something flashes in his eyes. I can't tell what it is, but his voice is softer when he speaks. "No, Mercy. I can't. That's not my call."

All I really hear is the "no."

I see him shaking his head, stepping back a bit, and I feel my stomach flip over. I drop my arms from around myself and clench my fingers into fists. The panic is rapidly being replaced with anger, and that's a good thing, actually.

I'm better with anger than I am with fear.

"I thought you gave a shit," I snap, my words tipped with venom.

Without saying anything else, I spin on my heel and march away, leaving him standing in the corner looking surprised.

My jaw tightens, and I blink back tears as I jostle my way through the crowd.

Goddammit. I thought they were starting to care about me, at least a little, but obviously I was fucking wrong. It's always been about their precious gang, about maintaining the Black Rose name and obeying orders. That's the only thing that matters to them. I've just been something fun to fuck around with in the meantime, clearly.

All the laughs and teasing and heated looks are just bullshit that means nothing in the end. Because I don't matter to them, and I've been so fucking stupid for thinking that I do.

I wish I hadn't set my drink down before, because suddenly all I want is something to take the edge off. All I can think about is my worry and fear for my dad and how no one will lift a finger to help him. I'm scared and pissed off, and I just need something to soothe the raw edges of my nerves.

The bar is packed with people, and I can't stand the thought of waiting in that crush to get a drink, so I wander the house instead, adrenaline buzzing through my veins.

Near the back of the large house, I step into a room that's dimly lit, and a pretty woman in a blue dress smiles at me.

"Hey. You want a drink?" she asks, holding up a crystal cut glass toward me like some kind of guardian angel of alcohol, here to save me from my own thoughts.

"Fuck, yes." I take the glass from her, relieved. I don't even know what's in it, but it's clear and it smells like booze, so that's good enough for me at the moment. I nod to her and lift the cup in a cheers before downing it in three quick gulps.

I barely taste it as it goes down, and I can only hope the buzz and haze of being a little drunk will set in soon. My heart is aching, already cracking at the edges as the echo of my dad's voice plays in my ears, and I need something to numb the pain before I do something I can't take back.

Please don't die, Dad. Please don't fucking die.

21

IT TAKES LESS than a minute for the alcohol to hit me like a semi truck, hot and burning as it kicks me in the gut. My head spins a little, but it's not the same feeling that I'm used to getting from alcohol. Not even from a strong drink, and the one I just chugged didn't smell like it was that strong.

There's a weird taste in the back of my throat, and just from the way I have trouble focusing all of a sudden, I know it can't just be the booze. Even with the drink and a half I already had, I wouldn't be feeling like this normally. Something else must've been in the cocktail she gave me, and I curse myself for being stupid enough to just throw something back without knowing what it was.

That's one of the first things my dad taught me when I started going to parties—never leave your drink unattended and never drink something if you don't know what it is. But in my haste to leave my anger and fear behind me, I didn't take the time to remember that.

I feel woozy, and I lean against the wall for a second, blinking as I try to force myself to focus on the girl who gave me the drink.

She's laughing, not in a cruel way, but in a way that makes it seem like we're both in on some joke.

"What the fuck was in that?" I manage to ask her without slurring my words too badly.

She lifts an eyebrow and shrugs. "It was just laced with a little molly. Just to get the party really going. Isn't that why you came in here?"

I shake my head, and it sends the world spinning again.

"Why wouldn't you get something from the bar if you just wanted a regular drink?" she asks, like *I'm* the idiot here. And maybe I am.

I push myself away from the wall, swearing under my breath as I do. My skin feels too hot, and everywhere the silken material of the dress rubs against me feels like it's exploding in sensation. I can't tell if it's a good sensation or not, to be honest, and I bite back a noise of frustration.

I try to make my way out of the room and through the crowd so I can get some air outside, but as I'm walking down the hall, I can feel the drugs really hitting me hard. The fact that I'm already at least two drinks in is definitely not helping, and I feel like no matter how hard I try to keep my feet on the ground and moving one step in front of the other, it's impossible for me to not feel like I'm floating.

My head is in the clouds, and the colors from people's clothes start to blur around the edges. It's like a rainbow of people, swirling and dancing, and I'm somewhere adrift in the middle of it.

I giggle at the idea of a bunch of gang members stretched out across the sky like a rainbow, stuck in place, glaring and angry about it. It's a funny image, and for a solid few seconds I can't stop laughing. Some people pass by and look at me funny, like I'm being weird, but I just keep moving past them, sometimes reaching out for the wall to help keep my balance.

There are so many people here. Fuck. *Too* many people.

When I get back to the main room, it almost feels like they're closing in on me. The music is too loud, the bass of it thumping through my body like a heartbeat, and the edges of the crowd seem to thump in closer with every pulse of the song. Someone brushes past me, and I startle hard, the slight contact radiating out from my forearm all the way down my fingers and up to my chest.

I can't tell if it's too much or not enough, and I lick my lips, my mouth suddenly so fucking dry.

All of a sudden, I feel very alone. That adrift feeling comes back, and I blink back a few tears. Goddammit. I'm *not* going to cry here. That would be stupid.

But everything and everyone feels so far away. I don't know any of these people. I want Scarlett. I want my dad. I want familiar faces and warm arms and someone to touch me with kindness.

If my dad dies, who will be left? Who will be my family?

It's all so fucking much. I feel like I can't breathe.

It feels like every one of my emotions are so close to the surface, making it impossible to ignore them as they all fight to be felt right away. The sadness, the loss, the fear, the anger, the strange feeling of arousal. It's all there, and I feel like the world is hurtling around me, making it so hard to hold on to anything.

I keep moving, trying to find a place to sit down or at least a place to lean where no one can touch me. I walk right into someone on my way to find a couch or something, and when I step back, the blurry form resolves itself into Sloan.

He opens his mouth and then frowns, looking down at me. Before I can brush past him, he grabs my shoulder.

"Look at me," he demands.

"Fuck off." I swat at him, trying to fight my way free, but he's too strong. He'd be stronger than me even if I weren't loopy as fuck, but if I were in my right mind, I'd have a decent chance of breaking his grip anyway. There's nothing I can do to get away from him in the state I'm in right now though. I can barely keep track of all my limbs, let alone use them to fight.

"Mercy DeLeon," he says, and my full name sounds so weird coming from him. Like hearing a teacher say your name on the weekend. Or something. I giggle in response, and he shakes me a little. "Hey. Look at me."

Finally, I glance up and nearly get lost in the thrashing storm of his eyes. They're so gray, so deep and a little dark. I forget to blink for a bit, and he stares right back at me.

"Are you drunk?" he demands, scowling.

I shake my head. Because I'm not. At least I don't think I am? I had drinks. But it's not the drinks.

Whatever Sloan sees in my face lets him know something is wrong, clearly, because he has that look on his face. That angry look like I've disappointed him.

In the mishmash of the feelings fighting for dominance in my chest, anger claws its way to the surface, flaring too hot and too bright. "Don't you fucking judge me," I say, and it's too loud to my own ears.

"What the fuck did you do?" Sloan shoots back, and I try to pull away from him again, but his fingers dig in harder. "Mercy, what did you do?"

"Get away from me," I snap. "You don't care. None of you. You don't fucking care!"

I can't control the words coming out of my mouth, and in the middle of the anger, I start feeling like I want to cry again. I rub my hands up and down my arms, and suddenly even my skin feels too tight. Everything is too much, and I want to lie in a cold, dark room for a little while.

Sloan keeps his hands on my shoulders and steers me away from the crowd. Rory and Levi materialize out of nowhere, and Sloan says something to them that I don't catch.

Whatever it is, it gets them to put their hands on me too, and I flinch away. "No," I mutter.

"Hey," Rory says. "You're okay. We're going to get you out of here."

"Wanna go home," I reply, sounding miserable.

They propel me a little faster out the door.

The air outside feels like a revelation against my heated face and skin, and I stop to drag in deep gulps of the fresh air. It's quieter out here, and the grass looks nice and soft. Like it would be a good place to lie down and take a little nap.

I start trying to head in that direction, but they won't let me. Of course they won't fucking let me. They never let me do anything I want to do. It's all what *they* want. Always what they want. I can't even lie down in the grass without Sloan pulling me back, trying to drag me off down the driveway to where the car is parked.

I struggle against his hold, and Rory steps in closer, helping him keep me close.

"Leave me alone!" The words pour from my lips over and over again. "Leave me the fuck alone!"

"We're going to take you home," Levi says, and I glance at him. His eyes are so brown. Like chocolate. Like velvet. "Let us take you home, okay? We'll take care of you."

I don't believe him. They sent my dad out there to die, and they won't do anything to help him. They don't care about him, and they obviously don't care about me. I can't trust them.

But I'm so tired. My limbs feel like they weigh a hundred pounds, and it's hard to even lift my legs to get in the car, so Sloan and Rory mostly lift me in.

Sloan takes the front seat, while Rory and Levi climb in the back with me, one of them on either side.

"What the fuck happened?" Levi asks once Sloan gets the car moving.

"She wouldn't tell me," Sloan replies darkly. "I don't know if she knows."

"Knowing the people at that party, could have been anything," Rory chimes in with a sigh.

Their words sort of go over my head, drifting in and out of my ears as the drugs kick in even harder. It's unbearable to be sitting in the stifling car, and the halter neck of my dress feels like it's choking me.

If I don't get this dress off, I feel like I won't be able to breathe, and I reach around to the back for the zipper, trying to get it off.

"Mercy, no," Levi says, batting my hands away. "Keep your clothes on."

"It's too fucking hot," I complain, moving away from him and closer to Rory. "Stop it. It's my dress, and I'll take it off if I fucking want to. You're not my fucking boss."

Giving up on the zipper, I manage to get the tie around the neck undone. The top of the dress falls down easily, the silky material slithering down my skin. I don't have on a bra under it, because the neckline and back are too dramatically plunging for that, so as soon as the fabric falls down, it exposes my bare tits to the car.

"Fuck," Sloan hisses, and I can see him looking in the rearview mirror. He drives even faster.

Levi and Rory are affected too, their eyes going dark. Rory licks his lips and glances away and Levi clenches his hands into fists in his lap.

We get back to the house in record time, and it feels like I blinked and we're already there. The two guys in the back help get me inside, pulling my dress back up to cover my tits.

When I glance at Sloan, he looks hard and closed off. He's mad, but it's nothing like the way he was the last time I embarrassed him or whatever while we were out. He turns away from me, like he doesn't want to look at me, and I look at the floor, breathing hard even though I don't really have a reason to be out of breath.

I don't know what to say to him, and it doesn't really matter one way or another, because he turns and disappears into the kitchen without another word, leaving the three of us alone in the living room.

Levi and Rory practically cart me up the stairs between them, and Rory pushes open the door to my bedroom so Levi can get me through. It's still a little bit of a mess from when I got ready for the party earlier, and if I wasn't so out of it, I might be embarrassed for them to see it. As it is, I don't give a shit.

"I've got it from here," Levi says, finally letting me go.

Rory hesitates, glancing from his friend then back to me, and it looks like he's unsure about leaving.

Levi just rolls his eyes and makes a face. "I'll take care of her," he says firmly. "I'm not a fucking prick. I'm not going to do anything to her."

"Yeah, I know," Rory replies. He moves to stand in front of me, reaching up to brush a few stray strands of hair out of my face. "You're gonna be okay?"

It sounds more like a question than when he said it before. As if he really wants to know the answer. Rory's nice. He cares. He *pretends* to care.

"I'm fine," I tell him, and he grins.

"That's our Hurricane." He leans in and gives me a quick peck on the lips and is gone before I can react to it.

Levi closes the door behind Rory and starts rummaging through my clothes in the dresser. He pulls out a pair of soft shorts and a t-shirt and puts them on the bed.

"Okay," he says. "Let's get your dress off."

"Let's get *your* dress off," I mutter back, and he shakes his head, coming to stand behind me.

His hands are warm as they ghost down my mostly bare back, fingers finding the zipper and dragging it down. He unties the halter top straps again, and the dress slides down my body and pools on the floor, leaving me in just my heels and panties.

I can tell Levi is trying hard not to look. He keeps his eyes focused on my hands as he holds one and helps me step out of the puddle of red fabric. He turns to get my t-shirt, and I step closer, running my hands up his back.

It's broad and strong and just as warm as his hands. I pull the hem of the shirt out of his nice pants, but if I want to get the shirt off, and I suddenly very much do, he's going to have to turn around. The thought of rubbing my naked skin against his naked skin is a very good one, and I make a soft noise of want just from thinking about it.

There's a sharp intake of breath from Levi, either at my closeness or the noise, and he turns around quickly. My fingers go straight for his buttons, but he catches my wrists in one of his large hands before I can make any headway.

"Mercy." His voice is low and firm. "No."

I pout and let him push me away, giving himself some space. In the back of my mind, I'm still upset about everything. My dad is out there somewhere, scared and feeling like he's going to die, and none of the guys will help him.

The feelings churning in my chest haven't gone away.

Emptiness, loneliness, guilt, and fear all claw at the inside of my rib cage, and I need something to make me feel better.

A good fuck would go a long way there. The heat and pleasure of it would chase away the bad feelings still festering in me, and I already know how good it can be with Levi. I know how solidly built he is under that shirt, and how good his dick is.

"Come on," he says, keeping me at arm's length. "Get dressed so you can get in bed."

"No," I mumble, folding my arms. "I don't want to."

He sighs with feeling. "Mercy. You can't go to bed in your underwear and heels. You need to put something on."

Fine. If he doesn't want me to sleep in my underwear and heels, then I won't. I shimmy my panties down my hips, letting them fall to the floor in a heap. Keeping my eyes on him, I kick off the heels and stand next to the bed, butt naked in front of him.

Levi just sighs again. "Good. Great. Get into bed, okay? You need to sleep this off."

I feel too keyed up to sleep, but lying down does sound nice, and the sheets are cool under my bare legs when I give in and sit down, so maybe it's not a terrible idea.

I kick the covers down, and Levi leans over to pull them up around me, but before he can, I grab his arm and drag him down on top of me.

He blinks for a second and then pulls away quickly. "Fuck."

"Sorry," I say with a little chuckle, even though I'm not.

He presses his lips together. He looks frustrated and tense, and I half expect him to leave and decide it's not worth it to put up with me when I'm like this. It wouldn't surprise me. They didn't sign up for babysitting when they said they would watch me, and if I choked on my own vomit or whatever in the night, it would be my own fault and one less problem for them to worry about.

I grit my teeth, waiting for Levi to shove off the bed and leave me, but he doesn't. Instead he moves to the other side of the mattress with a sigh, putting some space between our bodies as he settles his head on one of the pillows.

When he speaks, his voice is a low mutter. "It's going to be a long fucking night."

22

DESPITE THE EVENTS of last night, I wake up pretty early in the morning.

The sun is shining through the window, falling right on my face the way it does when it's too early, and I take my time letting consciousness wash over me, processing everything. My head is much, much clearer than it was when I fell asleep, and I open my eyes slowly, waiting for the headache of being hungover to hit me.

The light slices right into my head through my eyes like I knew it would, but other than that, the hangover isn't as bad as I expected. I feel more alert than I did before that's for sure, and I can tell that awful feeling of being high and out of control is gone. Thank fuck for that. The feeling of wanting to crawl out of my own skin was horrible, and I can only remember it in flashes.

I breathe a sigh of relief at feeling normal and then

yawn. It's still early, and I fully plan to go back to sleep for a while before I have to go downstairs and face the guys. I can only imagine how that will go down, considering I don't know what I might have said to them while I was rolling. I stretch slowly and then shift like I'm going to turn over and go back to sleep when two things hit me in rapid succession.

The first is that I'm naked.

Totally, one hundred percent naked.

I'm not even wearing underwear, and I know I put some on when I was getting ready to go out last night. My heart kicks into overdrive, and then I notice the second thing.

Levi is in bed next to me.

He's asleep, lips parted slightly as he breathes deeply and evenly, and my mind races alongside my heart, trying to put together what the fuck might have happened last night.

I can barely remember getting back to the house, really. I remember Sloan being angry and them getting me into the car, but other than that, it's all kind of a blur. My stomach rolls when I think about it too hard, and I swallow, forcing myself to take a deep breath.

"What the fuck?" I say out loud, and that's enough to wake up Levi.

He blinks quickly, face scrunched up as he yawns, and

any other time I might have thought it was a cute look on him.

Any other time when I'm not freaking out about holes in my memory and being naked as fuck.

"What the fuck happened?" I demand, sitting up and wrapping an arm over my tits so he doesn't get any more of the free show he's been enjoying for however long.

"Nothing." His voice is rough with sleep, and he reaches up to run the fingers of one hand through his hair.

I narrow my eyes and search his face. He looks a little groggy with sleep, but his expression holds no hint of guilt or deception. Still, I don't know whether I believe him or not. I don't think I do.

"You just lay there all night and didn't touch me?" I ask. "Yeah, right. Why am I naked then?"

"Because you didn't want to put your fucking clothes on," he says, sounding exasperated. "Look under the covers."

"What?"

"Just do it."

I keep my eyes on him for a second, but then I do as he says, lifting the covers to look. He's not naked. The nice button-down shirt he had on from last night is gone, as are his shoes and socks, but he's still wearing his dark, expensive-looking jeans.

Oh. I blink and look up at him.

"Nothing happened? Really?"

He chuckles, and it's a low, sexy sound that makes me shiver. I'm suddenly very aware of the fact that I'm not wearing anything and he can see that.

"Really," he says. "You tried your fucking best to make me break my promise to take care of you. You started stripping and trying to rub yourself all over me, and like I said, you didn't want to put on your pajamas." He looks at me, his gaze softening a little. "But no, I'm not so hard up for pussy that I'll fuck someone who's rolling on E."

I make a face at the reminder of how stupid it was to just drink something from someone I didn't know with no idea what it was.

"Okay," I mumble, a little embarrassed. "Good. And... I'm sorry you had to deal with that shit."

His expression changes slightly. A moment of silence hangs between us, and he holds my gaze, his eyes trained on my face intently. There's something churning behind his dark brown irises, some emotion that's hard to identify.

"It's okay, Mercy. It's just... I wouldn't want my next time with you to happen like that, you know?"

Now *that* catches me off guard. I remember the time when he came into my room to kiss me and say he wanted more, and this is just further proof that he thinks about it. That he wants me.

He wants there to be another time between us, and he wants it to mean something.

It's a lot to take in this early in the morning, but I can't stop thinking about how good he's been. He slept here beside me all night and didn't make a move. Apparently I wanted him to, and I have a vague memory of it now that he's told me it happened, but he didn't give in. He fended me off and got me to bed, like a fucking gentleman.

Like someone who cares.

The bed shifts as he rolls to the side before sitting up and stretching. His hair is mussed from the pillow, and there are creases on the side of his face. He looks warm and touchable like this, like something I could actually have.

Because the truth is, he's not the only one who wants there to be another time between us. I can admit that much, even if it's just to myself.

As he stands, I reach out and catch his wrist, halting him in place. Levi looks down at me, and I shuffle in bed, going up on my knees to kneel in front of him on the bed. The blanket falls away, letting him see that I'm still totally naked.

His eyes roam over my body, and he groans at the sight.

My heart is pounding so hard and fast I can feel it slamming against my ribs.

I wait, breath held, wondering if he'll take the chance or push me away again, and I'm not disappointed when he uses my grip on his wrist to yank me toward him roughly, sending me crashing into his chest.

There's a split second of hesitation as our gazes meet, and then we both move for each other at the same time, lips finding each other's in a hard kiss. I know there are probably still traces of the drug in my system, but I also know that has nothing to do with why it feels so good to kiss him like this.

Heat spreads through me, slow and syrupy, and I moan softly into his mouth, arching up and urging him to take the kiss deeper.

He takes the opportunity, slipping his tongue into my mouth and laying claim there in bold, swift strokes against my tongue. His hands roam down my body, sliding down my back and then lower so he can cup my ass.

The heat is almost searing, and I have the ghost of a memory of him unzipping my dress and the way I wanted his hands on me last night. This is so much better, though. I'm fully aware of everything that's happening, and I can feel the tightening in my core when he squeezes my ass hard, spreading me open for him just a bit.

I wait with a held breath, hoping he plans to touch me where I want to be touched the most, but instead he moves his hands back up, bringing them around to the front to slide into the sliver of space between us and cup my tits.

With a soft noise of pleasure, I arch forward, pushing them more firmly into his hands. My nipples are hard and pebbled, sensitive and aching when they stroke over the slightly rough skin of his palms.

"Fuck," he breathes against my lips, sounding almost tortured as he touches me.

A second later, he leans back from the kiss to look down at his hands, watching as his fingers stroke over the soft skin of my breasts and then find my nipples, tweaking them and making me gasp.

"I remember you like that," he says, and the raspy quality of his voice makes the declaration even sexier. "I pulled and twisted your nipples, and you almost came on the spot last time."

I swallow hard, because fuck, he's not wrong. I can remember it too, way more vividly than is probably healthy. I remember the way he played my body like an instrument, making me rise to meet his challenges and rewarding me for it by making me come again and again.

"I still like it," I breathe back, eyes dark as I look up at him. "I can take a little rough handling."

He snorts and pinches one nipple between his fingers. "I know you can. There's nothing fragile about you."

I moan and lean back a bit so that my nipple pulls against his hold on it, and the slight edge of pain there makes it feel even better. Levi's eyes flare with want, and he pulls me back in, kissing me again.

He bites down on my bottom lip hard, and I whine softly, sliding my hands down his chest and then down to his crotch.

I don't need to see his cock to know it's pulsing with heat, and that he's hard in his jeans. When he pulls back from the kiss again, Levi licks his lips and rolls his thumb over my other nipple, waiting to see what I'm going to do.

I know what I *want* to do, and for once, I don't over-think it. I undo the button and zipper on his jeans and work my hand down the front, feeling his hard, hot length against my palm.

He's big, I already know that, and I'm wet just thinking about it and how much I want him. How much I need him inside me. My pussy throbs with that need, my core aching and empty, and I wrap my fingers around his shaft, plas-tering myself against him.

His cock twitches in my hold, and I give in and start stroking him slowly, feeling the veins and ridges in his cock as I do.

Levi's eyes flutter closed for a second, and he licks his lips. "Fuck, Mercy. Your hand fits so perfectly around my cock. That feels fucking good."

I grin. The dirty praise makes me want to hear more, so I stroke him a bit harder, a bit faster, taking his cock from half hard to fully erect in just a couple of strokes.

Levi's breathing speeds up, and he groans, fingers digging into my hip when he uses it to hold on.

I like that sound. Fuck, I *really* like that sound.

It's so clear that he likes what I'm doing and wants me to do more, and I want that too. I don't want to just remember what it was like to be with him. Don't want to imagine it.

I want to experience it again, to feel all of it right here and now.

My heart pounds out a quick rhythm in my chest as I undo his pants all the way and then shove them down his legs along with his boxers, letting his cock spring free. It's long and hard, thick and flushed with need the way I feel. There's a moment where I just look at it, like I'm trying to memorize the size and shape, and my mouth waters at the prospect of tasting him.

I lick my lips, glance up at him once, and then decide to just go for it. He can stop me if he doesn't want it, but I'm pretty sure it's not going to be a problem.

The low, heated "fuck," that spills out of his mouth when I duck my head down and press a kiss to the base of his cock pretty much proves my point, and I smirk, pleased and determined to get more of those sounds from him before I'm done here.

I take my time, licking up his cock from base to tip, letting my tongue savor the musky taste of his skin. There's already a salty drop leaking from the small slit at the head of his dick, the precum that spills onto my tongue and proves how much he wants this.

I wrap my hand around the base of his cock and ease my mouth over the tip, sucking shallowly to begin with. It's been a while since the last time I did this, and Levi is definitely bigger than some of the other men I've been with.

But it's a challenge, and I never back down from those,

especially not when the reward for meeting this particular challenge is getting to see that heat flaring in Levi's brown eyes and the pleasure playing over his face.

He tangles his fingers in my hair after a second or two but doesn't force me down further. Instead, he just holds on, his breath coming out a bit ragged as I swirl my tongue around his dick and alternate between teasing him like that and sucking with intent.

His cock is warm and heavy in my mouth, and I hum softly around him, feeling the shudder of pleasure that goes through him at the sensation.

Gradually I find a rhythm, sucking him down deeper and holding for a second before working my way back up. Levi's hand in my hair is a welcome tether, another point of contact between us as I work him over with my mouth. He seems content to let me go at my own pace, gazing down at me with hooded eyes.

"Shit, Mercy. You're so good," he moans softly, stroking my hair a little. "Knew your mouth would be good for more than making smart-ass comments."

I snort in amusement and retaliate for *his* smart-ass comment by taking him down even deeper. There's a second or two where it's uncomfortable and I nearly gag and have to pull back, but I swallow through it, determined.

I'm rewarded by a choked off moan and his fingers going tight in my hair, which makes me smirk around him.

I take him deep again and swallow around his length, and I can feel the twitch in his cock.

If he wants to tease me about being good with my mouth, then I'll show him just how good I can be. I don't want him to come in my mouth, especially if that means he can't fuck me right away, but I want to make him feel good.

The sounds he makes and the way he keeps a hold of my hair go a long way toward upping my arousal too. I can feel that burning need at the center of my core, spreading out to my legs and arms, making me one big bundle of *want*.

My nipples are still hard and sensitive, and my pussy throbs with the desire to be touched, but I ignore them, focusing on the task at hand. I want to show Levi how good I can make it for him, in the hopes that he'll answer my challenge by making it good for me in turn.

I work my way all the way down, the head of his cock hitting the back of my throat and then slipping in deeper. This time I'm ready for it, and I stay there for a second, holding him in place.

"Fuck." Levi curses low again, and I roll my eyes upward so I can see his face. His eyes are closed, pleasure clear to see across his features, and there's an answering hum of that same deep pleasure in me.

I slide my lips back up his length to snatch a few breaths before I continue my onslaught, but before I can, Levi uses his hold on my hair to drag me all the way off his cock. A string of saliva trails between my lips and his cock head, and I gasp for air a bit, blinking up at him.

"Jesus. You're fucking good at that," he murmurs, panting slightly as he gazes down at me. "But I have other plans for you."

With that, he tosses me back, sending me sprawling onto the bed on my back, legs spread open. There's no way to hide from him, and I don't want to. He can see how wet I am, how swollen and slick my pussy is, ready and eager for him to slip inside.

For a second he just stares, like he wants to take it all in and memorize the sight, and then he moves, sliding his pants the rest of the way down and kicking them off. Then he's naked and crawling on top of me.

He's not quite as broadly muscular as Rory, but he's definitely well-built, and I have to stare at him for a second, just feasting my eyes on how damn sexy he is.

Every inch of him is toned and perfect, and when he finally lowers himself down so he's pressed skin to skin with me, it's a fucking amazing feeling. Heat and want shoot through me like electricity, and I wrap my arms around his neck, leaning up to meet him in a bruising kiss.

There's no question about what we both want at this point. I can feel his cock, hot and slick from my mouth, pressed against my thigh. He grinds against me slowly, and my pussy continues to throb, wanting him inside already.

"Please," I manage to get out, panting into the kiss. I

thread my fingers into the hair at the nape of his neck and arch, trying to get his cock exactly where I want it.

Levi just grins and reaches between us, grabbing hold of his dick and lining it up with my entrance. I think he's going to push inside, but instead, he rubs the hard length against my slit, teasing me and working me up even more.

I can't help the whine that spills out of me, or the way I buck up, grinding against him, trying to coax him inside of me. He just laughs, obviously enjoying himself. The head of his cock catches on the wet apex of my entrance, and I gasp sharply. I'm desperate to feel the stretch and slide of him entering me, but he rubs that tip around my hole instead.

"Stop fucking around," I groan, spreading my legs even wider.

"You want me that bad?" he asks, which is a pretty stupid question considering how I'm breathless and panting with need under him. "Tell me," he murmurs, dipping low once more to kiss me again.

He thrusts his tongue into my mouth, doing there what he's not doing to my pussy. I let my tongue tangle with his for a moment and then draw back enough that I can speak.

"Fuck me."

It's a demand, plain and simple, but I've never been the type to end up begging when I'm needy. Instead, I'm more than willing to make demands and take control if I have to, to get what I want.

Levi chuckles against my lips, and then he finally relents.

There's no more teasing. No more fucking around. Instead, he drives into me hard enough that it steals my breath for a second. My mouth drops open, and I clench my fingers in his hair, breathing hard while my body acclimates to feeling him so full and thick inside me.

"Is this what you wanted?" His voice is rough and gravelly. He pushes himself up onto his arms, hovering above me enough to have leverage for the next hard thrust.

All I can do is nod because it is. It's what I've wanted ever since the night he told me he wanted more from me. Probably before that, if I'm being honest. Definitely before that.

It feels so good, and he's not gentle or slow as he fucks me. His pace is fast and deep, driving his cock into me in thrusts that rock me and the bed with each stroke.

I hold on to him and take it, not even trying to hold back the sounds of my pleasure. I don't think I could even if I wanted to, honestly. It's just too good, especially after a dry spell, and it's not too long before I can feel the familiar flush of pulsing heat start to spread through me, bringing me closer and closer to the edge.

I clench tighter around him, breath catching, but Levi doesn't slow down. He just grins down at me and keeps working his hips, each hard thrust sending our bodies snapping together with the slap of skin on skin.

One of my hands slides to his shoulder, needing something to hold on to, and the other one slides down my own body, fingers teasing over my collar bones and down my chest to tweak my nipples, sending little sparks of pleasure bounding up my spine with each touch.

"Are you close?" Levi asks, chocolate brown eyes even darker than usual as he stares down at me. "Are you gonna come for me, Mercy? Gonna make a mess all over my cock?"

I can't hold back my whimper or find the words to answer him, so instead, I just nod. I can feel my orgasm building, starting small and slow but gathering steam as Levi keeps moving. His cock hits just right, pushing into the perfect spot inside me over and over again, and it's just a matter of time before I'm losing it for him, mouth dropping open as my ragged cry fills the room.

"Fuck! Levi!"

My shout ends on a moan, his name sweet on my lips as I ride out my orgasm. He doesn't even slow down for a second, fucking me into the mattress until I'm almost oversensitive, panting for breath and nearly boneless on the bed.

But it's clear he's not done with me yet. For one thing, he's still rock hard where he's buried inside me, and when he pulls out entirely, I can see his cock, dark and slick with our combined arousal. Even the slide of his cock leaving my body is enough to have me shuddering at the sensation, and he reaches for me, pulling me up and shifting our positions until he's flat on his back and I'm straddling him.

The view is just as good from on top, maybe even better. With the way the light hits his face, I can see the slight hints of lighter brown in his deep brown irises, and the way he looks at me leaves no question about what he wants.

Even breathing hard and sensitive from my first orgasm, I want more. I can't get enough of him, and I'm definitely not going to be satisfied until he comes too.

I tease him a bit, getting my revenge for his teasing earlier, working my hand slowly up his slick cock. I brush my thumb over the head of it and then smile when his dick twitches and his hips lift up on the bed.

"Now who's being a tease?" he asks, breathless, and I laugh.

"Turnabout is fair play, Levi."

But I'm not strong enough to make either of us wait any longer. My hand returns to the base of his cock, steadying it a bit, and I sink down onto it.

The new angle is different, but fuck, it's no less delicious. My head tips back at the way it feels to be fully seated on that dick, and I take a second to breathe through the torrent of feeling that threatens to sweep me up and carry me off.

Now that I've adjusted to his size, it's easy enough to

start riding him, my hands going to his chest to give myself some leverage for raising and lowering my hips.

Levi meets me in the middle, his hands on my hips, holding me tight. It's a compromise between me doing the work and him dragging me down into each thrust, turning our hot and sweaty fuck into a team effort.

His face is as flushed as mine feels, and I curl my fingers a bit, nails biting into the skin of his chest. The moan I get in response to that makes it clear he likes it.

The bed squeaks and groans under us as I feel a wave of pleasure rising once more. The aftershocks of my first orgasm have barely ebbed away, and already, I can feel another one on its heels. I fuck him faster, harder, my movements shifting from lifting my hips to rolling them in undulating waves that keep his cock buried so deep inside me.

"Levi," I moan, my mouth falling open as I fight for breath. "Fuck. Oh my god."

"Yeah, Mercy. Just like that." He urges me on, one hand staying on my hip while the other comes up to tease my nipples, tweaking and tugging at them. "Just like that, baby. You look so good like this. Taking my cock like you were made for it. Can you come again for me?"

The combination of his words and the way I'm basically grinding his dick into my sweet spot, not letting up on the constant stream of pleasure, is enough to have me right there on the edge, my entire body flushed with a tingling warmth.

Levi pinches my nipple hard, and I nearly scream from how good it feels, sensation traveling from my chest all the way down to light a fire in my core. I grind down harder on him, the movement pressing my clit down and adding friction right where I want it.

"Close," I manage to say, my eyelids drooping closed.

"Look at me," Levi breathes back. "I want to see it."

There's no way to resist him, and I snap my eyes open just as my orgasm crests to a peak. We lock gazes as I shudder my way through it, moaning his name, not giving a single shit about who might hear as the heat of my climax sears through me.

I'm still reeling from the pleasure of it all, my head nice and fuzzy with the overload of sensation, but Levi isn't done yet. He sits up enough that he can shift my weight back, pushing me onto my back again.

I lie there beneath him, blinking up at his face while he smirks and then leans down to kiss me. As soon as our lips meet, he drives into me hard enough that I cry out into the kiss.

It's messy, teeth and tongues clashing while I hold on to him, my legs going around his waist while he fucks me without mercy.

It's hard and fast, and I can tell he's getting close. I can't come again, but it still feels so damn good, and my body is wet and pliable for him, letting him use me for his own pleasure as he chases his release.

I arch up into each thrust, squeezing the muscles of my pussy to clench hard around him, dragging him in deeper every time he thrusts into me.

"Goddamn, Mercy," he groans, and I can feel the tremors in his arms where he holds himself above me. He's close to coming apart, and I want to see it.

I want to be the *cause* of it.

His breath comes in ragged pants, ghosting across my face as he leans in close enough that our mouths are just a hair's breadth apart. His hips keep driving forward, burying his cock inside me again and again.

"Shit. You feel so fucking good," he pants, kissing me again.

I can feel the desperation in it, the way his body is coiling tighter and tighter as he gets closer to losing it. I want that. I want to see the pleasure on his face when he falls apart and know that I'm responsible for it. I want to know that he's just as affected by how good this is as I am.

"Come on," I murmur against his lips, my legs tightened around his waist as I coax him in deeper. "Let me feel you. Fuck—Levi."

"Yeah," he breathes back. "God, yeah. I'm so close, Mercy. I'm gonna—"

His breath hitches on the end of that sentence, but I

can feel the shudders running through him, and I know full well what he was going to say.

His cock pistons in and out of me, slamming in deep enough that I can feel it all through my body. If I had another orgasm in me, I'd be already coming on his cock again, losing myself to how good it feels. Instead I drop my legs from around his waist so he has more room to move, and let him fuck me until he finds his climax.

It doesn't take long. There's a hitch in his breathing, and he slams into me a few more times before he pulls out suddenly. My pussy clenches around nothing, clearly missing the hot thickness of him inside me, but then Levi is fisting his own cock in short strokes. I watch, eager to see him find his release, and with a muted curse he does, splattering my stomach with his cum.

I guess I do have another orgasm in me, because a jolt of unexpected pleasure tears through me at the sight of him jerking himself off above me. It's not as strong as my first two, but it washes through me in a rising wave, making me shudder beneath him.

His chest heaves as he breathes through the last of his release, his cock slowly softening in his hand until he's completely spent. A soft groan of satisfaction pours from his lips, and I can't help the echoing noise that rises in my throat. He strokes his cock one last time, his hips jerking slightly, then buries his face in my shoulder.

I can feel him panting, his heart racing as we both come down from the high, and it's a damn good feeling.

"Was that what you had in mind?" I ask, my voice a bit ragged. "When you thought about us doing this again?"

He laughs softly. "Close enough, to be honest. Just as good as I imagined it being. Better."

Levi takes a few minutes to recover himself, and then he pushes back up onto his arms. For a second, I worry that he's about to leave now that he has what he came for, but instead, he slips off the bed and goes into my bathroom, coming back out with a towel. With a little smile on his face, he starts cleaning me up, hovering over me while he wipes the cum off my stomach.

It's a good angle for a kiss, and when he leans down to claim one, I lean up, meeting him halfway. The warm, sated feeling of the post-sex high is already stealing over me, and it mingles with something softer.

Something *sweeter*.

Something a whole hell of a lot more dangerous.

23

"FUCK, THAT WAS GOOD."

I say it out loud before I can stop myself, and then shrug mentally because, whatever. It's true, and I'm pretty sure Levi knows it as well as I do.

There's a satisfied look on his face while he cleans his cum from my stomach, and he laughs at the declaration, tossing the towel off to the side with his clothes and flopping back down on the bed beside me.

I didn't realize how much I needed something like that until it happened.

I've been keyed up for weeks, running on a cocktail of anxiety and stress since the last time I saw my dad, and finally I feel relaxed and sated in a way that's more than just surface level. I feel like if I let myself, I could melt into the bed and stay here for the rest of the day.

When Levi kisses me, I kiss him back, reaching up to thread my fingers into his hair for a second as our lips meet.

It's a sweet kiss, a short one that isn't meant to lead to anything, just something to top off the amazing sex we just had. It's easy to forget about everything else in this moment. To focus only on the way he feels against me, his lips on mine, the warmth between us as it grows and spreads out.

When I let him go, he rolls onto his side and pulls me closer to him, tangling our legs together. His hands roam my body, stroking over my shoulders and down my back. They seem hungry, like he can't get enough of touching me, and I certainly don't have any complaints about it.

We're quiet for a bit, relaxed and still in the afterglow. I let my fingers trail down his side slowly, feeling his warm skin while I trace the dips and angles of his muscles.

After a few minutes, he clears his throat a bit. "I know why you got so fucked up last night," he murmurs, his voice as soft as his touch. "You were pissed. And I get why."

I lick my lips, surprised that he brought it up. I'm even more surprised that he claims to understand, considering how adamant he was last night that there was nothing he could do.

I haven't talked about my dad with any of the guys since I've been here. Scarlett knows what he means to me, but she's known me for most of my life, so of course she does. Talking about it with the guys up until now has seemed... dangerous. Like if they knew what it all meant to me, they would be even quicker to take it all away and make sure I never see him again.

But I don't know if I believe that anymore. Levi is here, his hands on me, his eyes soft, telling me he understands. And I trust him a bit more than I would have otherwise. It's not like he's Sloan, with his hard expression and grumpy as fuck attitude and refusal to listen to anyone.

"It's just..." The words come out before I can stop them, and I decide to just go with it. Maybe it's the feeling of openness that comes after sex, or maybe it's the connection that seems to exist between us, whether I want it to or not. Maybe I just really want to talk about my dad to someone, so I can feel closer to him. I don't know. Either way, I keep talking.

"It's just that he's all I have," I tell Levi. "And I'm all he has. It's just been the two of us since my mom died. He's a good dad, and he loves me, but I know he hasn't had it easy. He's had to bust his ass and struggle and sacrifice for me, so I wouldn't have to do any of those things. If I asked him for something, he tried to make sure I could have it, and he taught me everything I know about being a strong person. He never made me feel like my options were limited because I'm a girl or whatever. He just told me if I believed in myself, I could do anything. I miss him. And I hate the idea that he could be in trouble because of all of this, and there's nothing I can do to help him. I don't even know where he is, Levi. I don't know if he's okay. He called last night, and I could tell he was scared and alone, and the whole time he was just trying to make sure *I* was all right."

It all comes pouring out of me, and I realize I must have really needed to say those words for a while now. This is the longest that I've been away from my dad in years, the longest time I've gone without having him there to turn to, to talk to and laugh with.

All of our little rituals have fallen by the wayside. Me sneaking into the locker room to cheer him on and give him a good luck pep talk. The two of us relaxing in our little living room with the sunken in couch to watch sports on the weekend, sharing plates of chicken wings and nachos between us. The jokes he used to make whenever I got dressed up to go out with Scar about how he thought he was raising a hellion not a proper lady.

I miss all of it, and it's been so weird to have it ripped from my life with no end to our separation in sight.

Whatever he's mixed up in, I have no way of knowing how it's going to change our lives. Maybe things will never go back to normal. Maybe all those rituals and jokes are gone forever. It makes me so sad to think about it, and it must show on my face because Levi's hands tighten on me for a second.

He sighs and pulls one of his hands back from my hip to drag it through his hair. He looks conflicted for a second, like he's debating with himself, but then sets his jaw. "I shouldn't tell you this, I really shouldn't. But... the thing with your dad is bigger than we knew at first."

"What do you mean?" I ask, frowning.

"We thought that he had just fucked us over by backing out of throwing the fight, but it turns out it wasn't just because of his own pride or whatever. That would have been bad enough, you know? Fucking over the Black Roses because you're too proud to lose one fight. Turns out, he was paid off by the Jackals and that's what made him double-cross us."

I blink for a second, shocked. "What the fuck? He took bribes from both gangs? And then fucked over the Black Roses?"

Jesus, why would he do that?

He must have known it would be suicide. There's no way he couldn't have known that. And why didn't he say anything to me about it?

None of it makes sense, and my head is spinning all over again, trying to come up with some reason that explains why he would put himself in danger like this. What could be worth that kind of risk?

"His match was actually a huge deal for us and the Jackals," Levi explains. "There's this church on the south side that's been sort of neutral territory for a while now. One of our gangs was going to claim it, and we bet on the fight. Winner got the church. So because your dad won, the Jackals won big, and shit has been unstable between us ever since then."

I know Levi is giving me information I'm not supposed to have, telling me things that could get him in trouble, but all it does is leave me with more questions than I had before.

Why Dad? Why that fight? Why would he choose to side with the Jackals, of all people?

Did they offer him more money? But what good does more money do if you're too dead to spend it?

"I just don't understand," I mutter, shaking my head. "I didn't know about any of this."

"Yeah. I figured you didn't." Levi grimaces slightly. "You're just here as collateral, not because we thought you were involved in any of it. Here's the thing, though. Right now, your dad is trapped between two gangs, which is a dangerous as fuck place to be. I'll see what I can do about keeping him safe and trying to get him out of this mess, but I'm not sure how that'll go. I'll do what I can to help though."

His face is open and honest as he talks, and I feel warmth swelling inside me. For the first time since this mess started, I don't feel like I'm trying to do this alone, and that's a feeling I want to cling to.

As if he's the physical embodiment of hope, I cling to Levi a bit too, leaning up to kiss him again. This time it has nothing to do with wanting to fuck or coasting on the lingering feelings of arousal.

I just kiss him because... I want to.

Levi leaves my room eventually, heading to his own room to shower and change.

I lie in bed alone for a little while longer, dozing on and off and thinking about all the things Levi told me. Eventually, I drag myself out of bed and into the shower to clean up. I want to wash last night off me, and standing naked under the hot water is a great reason to think about Levi's hands on me instead of anything else, even if there is a lot weighing on my mind at the moment.

I dry off and throw on some shorts and a t-shirt before heading downstairs to find something to eat.

After the shower, I feel more like myself. The queasy feeling of being drunk and high is gone, and I'm clear-headed, for the most part. My stomach is still a knotted mess, of course, anxiety clawing at me whenever I stop moving long enough to let it set in. I checked my phone after the shower, just to make sure I hadn't missed any calls or texts from Dad, but there was nothing.

I tried calling him, even though I wasn't sure it was a good idea since I don't know where he is or what he might be doing. But that worry hardly mattered anyway, because he didn't pick up.

I hope with everything I have inside me that last night wasn't the last time I'm going to hear from him, and whenever I think about that too hard, I kind of want to throw up.

My heart thuds dully in my chest. Instead of dwelling on those thoughts, I grab some veggies and meat from the fridge and start chopping them up, throwing together a quick stir fry.

As I cross back to the fridge to grab some ginger out of the crisper drawer, Rory walks in and comes to stand near me. He looks me up and down for a second and then searches my face like he's looking for something in particular.

I just gaze back at him, waiting for him to say something. Finally, he smiles a little.

"Are you okay?" he asks, and for once, there's no hint of teasing or flirting to be seen in his expression. It's weird to see him so serious. I've only seen him look like this once before, when he was discussing his daughter, but I nod.

"Yeah, I'm okay. Sorry if I was a bit of a mess last night. I was... fucked up about some things. After a good night's sleep and a shower, I feel like a new person."

"Right." He tugs his full bottom lip between his teeth, nodding a little.

There's a flash of something across his face, almost like disbelief but not quite, and it gives me the feeling that he knows there's more to my recovery than just sleeping and a shower. His room is right down the hall from mine, so it's entirely possible that he heard me fucking Levi this morning.

I'm not quite sure what to do with that, to be honest. I'm not ashamed of it, of course, and no one *made* him listen to us if that's the case, but it still feels odd, especially considering how close Rory and I have been growing over the last couple of weeks.

But working through those feelings in front of him seems like a very bad idea. So instead I just smile at him, barreling on ahead and ignoring the elephant in the room like I do best.

"I don't remember a lot about last night," I say. "But I do remember you were there."

"Well, yeah. We were all there," Rory replies. "And you were... definitely not yourself."

I make a face, because I don't even want to know what all I did last night. It's all fuzzy in my head, and if what Levi said about how I kept trying to get his clothes off and refusing to put mine on is true, who knows what I did before that?

"Yeah. I really wasn't. Anyway, thank you," I continue. "For being there and taking care of me last night. I remember you getting me in the car and up the stairs. I was a mess, and you weren't a dick about it, so... I appreciate that."

I eye him for a moment and then lean closer, going onto my toes so I can lean up and kiss him, just a light peck as a real thank you because I do appreciate it. Being out of it like that is dangerous, especially in the wrong company, and weeks ago, I *definitely* would've considered these guys the wrong company. But they didn't try anything, didn't take advantage of my fucked up state. They just brought me home and got me to bed, and that really does mean a lot.

My lips brush Rory's, and I go to pull back.

But before I can, he has his hands on my arms, holding me tight. He drags me in closer and deepens the kiss, mouth smashed against mine and tongue slipping into my mouth.

He kisses me like he has a purpose, and that purpose seems to be to get Levi out of my system.

Maybe I should fight it... but I don't. I *can't*. Not when I'm too busy melting into his kiss and making a soft noise of enjoyment that only seems to spur Rory on more.

With a graceful little movement, he turns us so he can push me right up against the fridge, almost slamming my back into it in a way that's more sexy than painful. I'm caught between the hard planes of his solid body and the refrigerator, and I know I'm not going anywhere until he's done with me.

The kiss turns deep and exploring, and my tongue darts out to dance with his. My eyes slip shut, and I let out a shuddering breath into the kiss that just makes him draw back enough that he can nip at my bottom lip with his teeth.

I suck in a short gasp at that, and he kisses the sting of it away before drawing back entirely, giving me room to breathe again.

Those green eyes of his roam over my face, taking it in. I'm sure my pupils are dilated. My face is definitely flushed, and my chest is heaving while I try to catch my breath after that soul-stealing kiss.

Rory just grins, and it's such a charming and sexy smile that it makes me want to drag him in for another kiss on top of the first one.

The smug asshole.

He nods in satisfaction and steps away completely, leaving me leaning weakly against the fridge.

"You're welcome," he says belatedly. And then he walks right out.

He doesn't make coffee or get a snack or anything, so clearly he came in here for the express purpose of flustering me in the middle of the day. It takes me a good few seconds to remember what I was even doing, and I'm glad I didn't turn on one of the stove burners before he came in and did all that.

I might have burned the fucking house down.

Trying to get my head on straight, I shake myself and push away from the fridge, opening it and staring inside for a second before I grab the ginger I was going for in the first place.

Fuck. One kiss wouldn't normally be enough to have me all scattered and distracted. Even if it was a really good kiss.

But nothing is *normal* when it comes to these three men and the way they manage to keep me continually off balance.

Shaking my head, I go back to slicing veggies, trying to focus on the task at hand so I don't accidentally chop my finger off or something, but my mind is a swirling mess of thoughts.

I thought I had a solid plan when I came to live in this house. I thought I could handle this shit. But between the phone call with my dad last night and everything that's happened since, I'm beginning to realize a terrifying truth.

I'm in way over my head here.

THE AFTERNOON PASSES IN A BLUR. It's been a weird day, all things considered, but definitely better than yesterday was.

My dad's phone call from last night still plays on repeat in my head, making my stomach churn. But at least I'm not drunk or high anymore. As painful and awful as it is to face reality, it's nice to be clearheaded and not rolling on drugs I didn't even mean to take.

In the late afternoon, I call to check in with Scarlett, lying on my bed and speaking in a low voice as I fill her in on everything. She seems as freaked out as I am by my dad's words, which I repeat back to her practically verbatim. They're seared into my memory, it feels like.

She knows my dad well. He practically raised her too, considering her own home life was pretty fucking shitty and she spent more time at our house than at hers when we were kids.

She knows how determined he is, and just like I do, she knows he wouldn't say the kind of things he said unless he really thought he might not make it. He wouldn't worry me for nothing.

But even though I can tell Scar is scared just like I am, she stays calm and tries to talk me off the ledge of panic, reminding me that my dad wins so often in the ring not just because he's strong, but because he's *smart*.

"Thanks, Scar," I murmur when we've talked it out as much as we can. "I love you."

"You too, hot stuff. It'll be okay."

We hang up, and I lie on the bed for a while, staring up at the ceiling. I take several deep breaths, letting a sort of calm wash over me.

I can still feel where Rory kissed me, still feel the pleasant soreness from fucking Levi, and for once I'm not freaking out about it. Levi's promised to help me figure out what's going on with my dad, and Rory hasn't really given me any reason to doubt him either.

They're both better men than I would have given them credit for when I first met them, and finally, that pit of anxiety in my stomach seems like it's starting to ease a little.

Maybe there's still a way out of this. Maybe it will be okay.

I need to talk to Sloan though. And that's... that's a kind of anxiety all of its own. Out of the three of them, he's the only one I haven't seen since last night. I remember him being pissed off when we got back to the house, but I can't tell if it was him being mad at me for making an idiot of myself in public again or him being angry at the situation. Or him just being pissed because he's Sloan, and he's always pissed.

He hasn't come to check on me, or ask if I'm doing better, which probably doesn't bode well, and my face heats as I sit alone in my room, thinking about the embarrassment I'm going to feel if he heard me fucking Levi too.

I'm not ashamed of it. We both wanted it, and we're both consenting adults. But still, I don't really want to face Sloan if he knows about it. I'm sure it'll just be another thing that'll make him irrationally angry.

Whatever Sloan's weird issue about me being around other guys is, I don't know if it extends to the men in this house. But if it does, that's his problem. I'm not going to stop myself from doing what I want just because he's got a stick up his ass and doesn't know how to communicate except through being a dick.

Rory kissed me like he wanted to be the only one I could taste, but somehow, I figure whatever Sloan's reaction is will be less pleasant.

But I *do* need to talk to him. He's the closest to the top of the hierarchy in the Black Roses. His dad is the leader, and if anyone knows what's going on, it'll be Sloan. I don't know what kind of sway he has with his father, but maybe he'll at the very least have some information I can use. Something to let me know that my dad is okay so that worry will stop eating a hole in my stomach like acid.

The real trick will be getting him to tell me if he *does* know something.

Of all of these men, Sloan's the one who's probably least likely to give up sensitive information. Maybe he has more riding on it, maybe it's a family loyalty thing, but I don't see it being easy. And I'm not sure he's the type to tell me what I want to know after a good fuck like Levi.

There was definitely nothing soft or open about the way we almost hooked up, weeks ago now, and it left him more closed off than he was before, if that's even possible.

I don't have a plan, really. I'm not sure what angle to go with or how to best get him to open up to me. The best thing I can think of is just to ask—to let him know it really means something to me and hope for the best.

It's not a very good plan, but it's all I've got when I leave my room and go looking for Sloan.

The house is pretty quiet, which isn't that weird for a Sunday. Rory must be with Piper and Jen, and Levi's probably downstairs in the gym. None of the guys track my movements that closely anymore. They've obviously realized I'm not going to run, and that they don't need to monitor me twenty-four seven.

I make my way down the hall, deciding to try Sloan's room first to see if he's there before I head downstairs to look.

As I get close to his room, I can hear his voice, raised slightly in conversation. No one answers him back that I can hear, so he must be on the phone.

My footsteps slow, and I reach out to rest a hand against the wall as I crane my neck a little.

His voice is low, and he's talking like he doesn't want to be overheard, but also like he's trying to convey some urgency to whoever he's talking to. There's no anger in his voice for once, but he sounds weird either way. Something about his tone makes me anxious to know what he's saying. I hold my breath and tiptoe a little closer, trying to see if I can figure out what he's talking about.

I can't tell who he's talking to just from his side of the conversation, and I frown, leaning closer to the door and hoping the floorboards won't creak beneath my feet and give me away.

"...time is up," he says. There's a slight pause. "Yes, I'm sure. I'll meet you soon. Same place as last time. Just be there."

He falls silent, and I can't tell if he's hung up the call or is listening to what the other person has to say about his declaration. I frown as I stand frozen, thinking hard.

There's a weird feeling in my stomach, and it isn't the constant anxiety I've been living with for once. It's more like when I decided to follow Rory, so sure that he was hiding something with his frequent solo trips away from the house.

Only I'm pretty sure with Sloan, it's not going to turn out that he has a secret family or anything like that.

This feels like something bigger, something more important.

It could be nothing. Maybe it's something totally innocuous, like him planning to get a gift for a friend or having some hobby he's embarrassed about. But somehow, I don't think so.

And there's only one way to find out.

He said he was going to meet someone, and I make a split-second decision to follow him wherever he's going. My dad's life could be on the line, and even though Levi said he would try to help, the one I *really* need to get on my side is Sloan.

Given how antagonistic our relationship has been so far, I don't think I'm going to win him over with a few nice words. He's the kind of guy who only responds to power, so that's what I need.

Power.

I need something I can hold over him. I need to know more about him.

My pulse counts down the seconds as I stand just inside the door to my bedroom, waiting to hear Sloan walk down the hall and descend the stairs.

This time, I'm much more careful when I tail him. I learned a thing or two when I followed Rory, and I am definitely more concerned about Sloan finding out I'm following him than I was about his easygoing friend.

I give him a bigger head start when he leaves in his car, and I stay farther back as I follow on my bike—far enough back that I risk losing him completely, blending in with the traffic more while keeping an eye on Sloan's car in the distance.

He's heading for the part of town that's under development, all empty lots and construction projects that are half finished or stalled for one reason or another, and that just ups my suspicion even more. It's not a shady part of town, definitely not as shady as the places the Black Roses usually hang out, but it's out of the way enough that it seems like the kind of place you'd go if you didn't want to be found or overheard. It's usually pretty deserted, considering there's nothing to do around there.

I let Sloan get a little more ahead of me, keeping track of the exit he takes and then taking it myself, weaving in and out of cars on my bike until I see him again heading down a side street. I catch up pretty quickly, watching from a distance as he pulls into an empty lot. His car idles for a bit before he cuts the engine, and then it's another couple of minutes before he gets out of the sleek black vehicle.

I hide behind one of the buildings across the street. It's

also empty, either waiting for someone to buy or lease space in it or for the city to decide to tear it down. There's a good view of the lot and Sloan's car, and I'm pretty confident he can't see me.

My heart is racing. Something's going to happen here, and the sour twist in my stomach tells me it's not going to be anything good.

Black Rose business can be grim, I know that much, and I really don't want to see Sloan kill anyone or do anything too violent, even though I know it probably won't be the first time he's had to do something like that in the name of the gang he's a part of. It probably doesn't even faze him anymore.

Sloan stands next to his car, drumming his fingers on the hood in an impatient gesture. Less than a minute later, someone steps out of the lengthening shadows on the far side of the lot and starts walking over to meet him.

It's a man, tall and broad, and when he gets close enough that the last rays of light catch his face, I clamp my lips tight around the gasp that almost escapes my mouth.

It's my dad.

HE'S ALIVE.

Thank fuck.

He looks tired and worn down, but it's him. Whole and healthy-ish, and standing right there. It's the closest he's been to me since I was taken away by the guys that night.

I want to rush out from my hiding spot and run to him. I want to throw my arms around his neck and breathe in the familiar scent of leather and sweat that I associate with him. I want to convince Sloan that he can let this go, that my dad can go home and rest and not have to face any more horrible consequences for what he did. I'm not sure why my dad double-crossed the Black Roses, but he doesn't deserve to die for it.

I don't do any of those things though. I stand still, rooted to the spot, and I watch. There's a flare of hope inside me though, a spark that burns in my chest. Maybe Levi talked to Sloan earlier. Maybe Sloan is going to help my dad somehow. Maybe, just maybe, he cares enough to do it without me asking.

For once, the hope crowds out the worry, and I clench my hands into fists, my heart drumming an insistent beat in my chest as I watch and wait to see what will happen.

Sloan nods a greeting, and my dad returns it.

Dad reaches up and drags fingers through his hair, his gaze darting around the empty lot like he half expects someone else to step out. He seems jumpier than usual, his hair a little longer and stubble on his jaw, and I can only imagine what he's been through these past several weeks.

The urge to run to him is still strong, and I keep ignoring it. If this works out and Sloan does something to help, then we'll be together soon anyway. I just have to be patient.

"I can't do it," Dad says. He's far enough away that I have to strain to hear his words, but even from this distance, I can pick out the exhaustion and fear in his voice. He laughs, but there's no humor in it at all. "I've been trying, believe me, I've been trying. But I haven't been able to do it. I need more time."

Sloan stands perfectly still, gazing at my dad and listening. There's a thoughtful look on his face, then he sighs. "That wasn't the deal."

"Yeah. I know it wasn't. I'm just telling you where I

stand. I can get it done with more time, I think, but right now..."

Dad trails off, and his posture seems to get a little more hunched.

It makes me angry to see it. My dad has never been the type to let life beat him down. Even losing my mom, the love of his life, didn't knock him down for very long. His heart never fully recovered, but he threw himself into taking care of me, making sure I had everything I could ever need or want, and working his ass off to take care of us both.

He was always laughing and teasing. Even with just the two of us, the house never felt empty or dull. There was so much laughter and love.

The man in front of me though? He seems like a stranger. Like my dad if he aged ten years overnight and lost that strength to his spine.

He seems... broken.

And there's nothing I can do to protect him from it.

"Come on, Sloan," I whisper inaudibly, more just moving my lips than anything.

I stare a hole into the side of his head, willing him to do something, offer some solution. Anything that will help. Even granting Dad more time so we can figure something out.

The way Sloan is standing, I can only make out his profile, but his expression makes it look like he's sorting through the options in his head. I hold my breath, waiting to see what he's going to say.

But in the end, he doesn't say anything.

Instead, he pulls a gun from the waistband of his jeans and aims it right at my dad.

Time seems to slow down.

There's no time for Dad to react, and Sloan's face is impassive. I feel like I can't breathe or move or do anything, frozen in place as Sloan pulls the trigger.

Not once, not twice, but three times in quick succession.

The gunshots echo around us, shattering the silence. There's no one around to hear them though. No one but us.

I watch as my dad's body jerks, each of the bullets hitting him with brutal force. Blood blooms and stains the shirt he's wearing, marking the places where he's been shot. There's no sound, but I *feel* it all the way through my body when he collapses, dropping to his knees and then crumpling to the pavement in a heap.

Sloan just stands there for a second, not moving, gun still raised, staring down at my dad's body. My heart lurches into my throat, and I feel like I'm going to be sick. I couldn't move if I wanted to, stuck still, trying to remember how to breathe.

After a few more seconds pass, Sloan finally moves. He grabs my dad by the ankles and starts dragging him to the car, lifting his body with a grunt of effort so he can dump it in the trunk.

He slams the trunk closed and then hops back in the car, peeling out of the lot and driving away.

It takes another couple of minutes for me to do anything other than stand with my hand pressed against the brick of the building beside me, staring after the car in shock. I feel cold and numb, and the last of the evening light starts to bleed away as I stand there.

Something urges me to move, so I do, running across the street and dropping to my knees in front of the spot where my dad fell. Blood stains the pavement, stark and red and impossible to look away from, even in the dying light.

I stare at the spot until my vision starts to blur with tears. There's a wheezing sound in my ears, and it takes me a second to realize it's me. My breathing is coming out in shallow gasps as I start to hyperventilate.

I can't even put a name to what I'm feeling, alternating between numb shock and some fucked up cocktail of every other negative emotion.

He's dead.

My dad is dead.

The man who raised me, who taught me everything I know. How to be strong, how to drive, how to fight. The only family I have left, shot dead and stuffed in a fucking trunk.

By Sloan. Just like that.

The hope I had just minutes ago feels like ashes in my mouth now, snuffed out by the reality of what just happened. I fall forward onto my hands and knees, trying to suck in gasps of air, but it's hard. My throat feels like it's got invisible hands wrapped around it, cutting off my air supply. Tears fall from my eyes, splattering on the asphalt, and my shoulders shake with silent sobs.

I keep replaying the scene over and over again in my head.

My dad's tired expression.

Sloan's thoughtful, almost impassive face.

The freeze-frame image of Sloan aiming his gun and my dad standing there, helpless.

I close my eyes, trying to block it out, but it's impossible to forget, so vivid and fresh.

I have no idea what Sloan plans to do with the body. Toss it in the river or bury it along with all the other bodies of people who ended up on the wrong side of the Black Roses? And then he'll be heading back to the house, to what? Tell the others what he did? Pretend like it didn't happen?

Either way, I have to be there when he gets back or he'll know I snuck out. He'll realize I followed him.

It's that thought that finally gets me moving. I manage to pick myself up off the pavement on shaky legs and stumble across the street back to my bike.

It's a good goddamn thing this part of town is so deserted, because if anyone saw me right now, they'd be worried I was deranged. That's how I feel when I throw my leg over my bike and start moving.

It's like I'm in a daze, confused and cold and trapped in my own head. I can barely remember the ride back to the house, autopilot taking over to hopefully help me obey traffic laws and not cause any accidents.

I feel like I'm walking in a dream when I stow my bike in the garage and sneak back in the house, finding it just as quiet as I left it.

It was only an hour or so ago when I was sneaking out, worried about what I was going to find when I followed Sloan but not expecting anything like what I actually saw.

I go to the kitchen and splash some cold water on my face, then fill a glass and chug it. The cold water almost burns going down, and it seems like another lifetime that I stood in this kitchen making out with Rory against the fridge.

Does he know? Did he know then? He seemed like he was more focused on what happened between me and Levi, but how do I know that's the case? Maybe he was thinking about how he knew they were going to kill my dad.

Fuck. *Fuck.*

There's so much I don't know. So much I have no way of finding out unless I come out and demand answers, and after seeing what Sloan did to Dad, that seems like a really fucking bad idea.

My head starts to clear from the daze I've been in since I saw my dad die, but panic starts setting in right on its heels. I leave the kitchen and start heading up the stairs toward my room when it hits me.

I shouldn't have come back.

I can't be here.

It's not safe.

I don't know what Levi and Rory know. I don't know if they're in on it or if this is a new plan or if this has *always* been the plan. My dad is fucking dead, and they could kill me next. Maybe I know too much. Maybe that was why Levi didn't have a problem telling me things this morning— because he knew I'd never be able to use the information anyway.

Unhelpfully, my brain starts supplying me with all kinds of scenarios that end with me dead and no one knowing. Maybe Scarlett would be able to figure out what happened, but what could she do about it?

She can't go up against the Black Roses on her own. It would be suicide. And the cops would be no fucking help.

My heart is going a mile a minute, and I'm not sure what to do. I can't stay here, but I don't know where to go. I should have just bolted after I watched Sloan...

After he...

Fuck. God. Fuck.

I can just go. Just *run*. Forget having a plan, forget finding a safe place. Anywhere has to be better than this, right? I can go to Scarlett's and hide out there, or better yet, skip town all together and not drag her any deeper into this mess with me. Maybe if I get far enough away, they won't be able to come after me.

It's probably wishful thinking. Everybody in this city fears the Black Roses for a reason—because people don't cross them and live. But empty hope is all I've got at the moment, so I cling to it with both fucking hands.

I take the stairs back down two at a time, but before I can make it through the living room, I hear the front door open.

"Your savior is here with pizza!"

It's Rory. The sound of his deep voice would usually calm me down, but instead, it makes my pulse kick into a wild gallop. I'm stuck in the middle of the living room looking like a deer in headlights.

"Savior my ass." Levi comes down the stairs, rolling his eyes. His hair is damp from a post-workout shower, and he looks comfortable in sweats and a t-shirt. When he sees me standing by the couch, he grins. "There you are. I'm sure you heard because he's a fucking loudmouth, but Rory brought pizza. We're gonna watch a dumb movie and eat. Come on."

He takes my hand and starts tugging me in the direction of the couch. It takes everything in me not to snatch my hand away from him, and I hate how just him touching me calms me down a little. Because I can't trust him. I can't trust either of them. I don't know what they want from me. I don't know what they know.

I feel like I'm drowning in worry and anxiety, and Levi seems totally casual and relaxed.

Rory walks into the living room, pizza boxes in hand, and he winks at me as he moves to set them on the table.

"Hey, Hurricane. Where do you fall on the pineapple on pizza debate?"

"The... what?" I stammer, blinking at him.

He can't be talking about something as mundane as pizza toppings right now. Not when my whole world feels like it was shattered apart less than an hour ago.

"Pineapple on pizza," he repeats, grinning. "I picked up a bacon and pineapple pizza because I know Sloan hates it. Figured it means there'll be more for the rest of us. Unless you're a heathen who's against a little sweet and salty action."

He leans closer to me, waggling his eyebrows, and I can hear the flirtatious undertone in his words. But it doesn't make me feel better. If anything, it makes that feeling in my gut worse. If he knows what's happening, then he's playing a sick game.

But he's also waiting for an answer, clearly, so I swallow hard and glance down at the boxes. "It's fine. I don't mind it."

"That's what I said," Levi chimes in. "Would I order it myself? Probably not. But if you put it in front of me, I'll eat it. Pizza is pizza."

"Okay, you say that, but what if I brought home something like ham and olives? Mushroom and anchovy? Green pepper and eggplant?"

"They don't have eggplant pizza."

"They do in Italy."

"Well, if we ever go to Italy, I'll worry about it then."

They banter back and forth the way they always do, and I just stand there until Levi gives me a look. Moving on some kind of autopilot, I go to sit next to him on the couch, my skin prickling with nerves.

My palms are sweaty, my fingers twitching to curl into fists. I can't decide if I should try to fight my way out of here or just bolt and make a run for it. And even as my mind plays out a half dozen different scenarios, the two men keep acting so fucking relaxed and normal that it's hard for me to focus. I feel like I'm going fucking crazy.

Rory brings plates and napkins from the kitchen and starts handing out slices. He puts one bacon and pineapple on my plate, and one pepperoni and sausage, and I take it, staring down at the little puddles of grease in the pepperoni cups. I'm not even a little bit hungry.

In fact, I think I might throw up.

"Where's Sloan?" Rory asks. "His car's not here."

As soon as the words are out of his mouth, the front

door opens again, and I go rigid, my stomach dropping to the floor.

"Speak of the devil." Rory grins, then cranes his neck to call over his shoulder. "Sloan, get in here! Pizza's getting cold."

"I'm coming." The deep voice floats toward us from the front of the house, and a second later, Sloan steps into the living room.

He looks exactly the same as he did when I saw him standing across from my dad, shooting him dead. There are no lines of tension in his posture, no look of remorse on his face. He looks totally casual. Like nothing even happened.

But it did. I fucking *saw* it. I can't stop seeing it in my mind's eye.

"Where were you?" Levi asks him, biting into a slice and sucking in air when it burns his tongue.

"Went to get coffee and check out that sale on TVs," he answers, lying through his fucking teeth. "They didn't have that big one we were talking about getting."

"Aw, damn." Rory grunts, settling back on the couch. "I knew we should have jumped on it earlier."

Sloan grabs a slice of pizza and a plate and drops down into the armchair, lifting an eyebrow at me when he catches me staring. I shift my attention quickly back to the pizza while Levi gets the movie going.

My earlier thoughts of running filter out of my mind,

vanishing like dust as I bore a hole in the slice of pizza with my gaze.

Something totally fucked up is happening here.

Sloan killed my dad, and now he's lying about it to his friends. So maybe they don't know. Maybe they're not in on it at all.

But then, *why?*

Levi and Rory are members of the gang too. Clearly, they know what's been going on with my dad up until now. So why lie to them? Why aren't they in the loop?

I should run. I should get up, throw this pizza down on their stupid, expensive couch and run away.

But I won't.

I can't.

Sitting here, watching Sloan out of the corner of my eye, all I feel is hatred. It's even stronger than it was when I first came here, burning like fire through my veins. I didn't know the meaning of the word "hate" until now. And now, that one paltry word doesn't seem like enough.

Whatever this feeling is that's burning in my chest, it's worse than hate.

Sloan killed my dad, and I want to destroy him. Destroy his entire family.

If I go to the cops, they won't be able to help. The Black Roses run too much of the city. They have a tight hold on businesses and even some local politicians. There are definitely at least a few cops in their pocket. I can't just show up and tell them about this. For one fucking thing, I have no proof. Just my word against Sloan's, and in this case, he has much, much more power than I do.

But I'm angry. I'm so fucking mad. Just sitting in the same room with that snake makes me seethe with rage. If I want to get my vengeance on him for what he did, I'm going to have to get it from the inside.

Which means no running.

I'm staying.

I'll play it cool, act like nothing has changed. I'll watch and I'll wait, and if I don't see an opening to take the Black Roses down, I'll *make* one. Because the stakes are higher now. I can't save my dad anymore, but I can at least get revenge for him.

I'll make Sloan wish he'd never fucked with either of us.

I'll make him fucking pay.

BOOKS BY EVA ASHWOOD

Clearwater University
(college-age enemies to lovers series)
Who Breaks First
Who Laughs Last
Who Falls Hardest

The Dark Elite
(dark mafia romance)
Vicious Kings
Ruthless Knights
Savage Queen

Slateview High
(dark high school bully romance)
Lost Boys
Wild Girl

Mad Love

**Sinners of Hawthorne University
(dark new adult romance)**
When Sinners Play
How Sinners Fight
What Sinners Love

**Black Rose Kisses
(dark new adult romance)**
Fight Dirty
Play Rough
TBA
TBA

(contemporary romance standalone)
Say Yes

**Magic Blessed Academy
(paranormal academy series)**
Gift of the Gods
Secret of the Gods
Wrath of the Gods

Printed in Great Britain
by Amazon

84651799R00174